ON
A
SCALE
OF
1 TO
1

ON A SCALE OF 1 TO 10

Ceylan Scott

Chicken House

SCHOLASTIC INC. / NEW YORK

TO MY MAMA

First published in the United Kingdom in 2018 by Chicken House, 2 Palmer Street, Frome, Somerset BA11 1DS.

Library of Congress Cataloging-in-Publication Data available

ISBN 978-1-338-32376-4

10 9 8 7 6 5 4 3 2 1   19 20 21 22 23

Printed in the U.S.A.   23

First edition, May 2019

Book design by Baily Crawford

THEN

The two girls had been drinking since three, a swig for every crash of the river. The Golden Virginia they were smoking like shriveled worms falling out of rolling paper. They tried to blow rings in the sticky air.

Failing.

Giggling.

Heads spinning. Could be the alcohol, could be the heat.

Now it was late, and the sky was pale pink, like the smooth inside of a conch. Cans of cider glinted in the grass and trees flopped like vast ivory wigs, heavy from the weeks of rain. Henna patterned the girls' bare arms, a memory of windswept festivals bleeding color.

The blonde girl swigged.

The second girl made daisy chains the lengths of her legs. She picked them up and threw them into the river, where they floated like tiny lilies. A crow leered over a piece of over-grilled bacon discarded from a barbecue. It squawked, its black eyes shining. The girls talked.

The first girl beckoned to the surging river ahead of them, brown and black and foaming. They laughed. The second girl nodded.

Their fingers interlocked in a drunken clasp and they swayed as they stood up. They didn't put any shoes on. The dam in front of them shouted.

"We're such idiots," said the blonde girl.

"Such idiots."

They stumbled over soapy tangles of moss and their calves turned pink with the cold. The branches of a dead tree sprawled like bones and the blonde girl's faded lilac streaks echoed the sunset.

"Jump, Iris," she said. "I'll follow you."

NOW

The first thing they do at Lime Grove is try to make me talk about the monster.

Dr. Flores and a nurse in a blue uniform, trying to hollow out the small scraps of truth, asking me one hundred questions in one hundred different ways in the hope that one will catch me out.

How did the self-harming start?

Will you tell us what happened?

You know your behavior isn't normal, don't you?

Let us help you.

Only you can help yourself.

How do you feel? On a scale of one to ten?

I don't talk. The monster won't let me. The room is decorated in a painful pink palette: cracked pink walls, pink metal cupboards, pink leather armchairs, and a forlorn-looking fuchsia beanbag chair in a corner. The sign on the door says it is THERAPY ROOM 1, which is stupid because I didn't see a Therapy Room 2 or 3 and this doesn't feel like therapy. Denim cradles my thighs but I'm shivering at the knees and my hair is dripping more grease than a deep-fat fryer. Angry spots have swollen around my lips. I don't know why.

Dr. Flores scribbles something down on his notepad, holding it at an angle so I can't read his spindly writing.

"Sorry, we have to take notes," he says. "It's standard practice."

Dr. Flores is lanky but short in all the wrong places. He chews his pen lid like gum and is wearing a three-piece suit, a stripy purple shirt, and a periodic table tie that knots perfectly around helium. He is wearing scratched, thick-rimmed glasses and lots of hair gel, which makes him look like a hedgehog. I get the impression he doesn't like me, but maybe it's just easier to distance yourself from the fate of a patient if you don't like them and they don't like you.

The nurse reeks of newly qualified. Her blue uniform is creased and new, her smile molded like clay.

"Let's have a think about how you felt when—"

"When can I go home?" My voice cracks more than I want it to.

"You have to stay here for an assessment."

"Assessment of what?"

Dr. Flores looks down at the bandages wrapped around my arm, the small, round Band-Aid where the cannula had pierced my hand, the bruise on my neck that looks like dark wine, and it's his turn not to answer.

"What happened to Iris?" he asks instead.

After an hour, he stops asking.

If you really want to know everything, the first thing I'll probably tell you is that growing up I lived in paradise and then it was shattered when I moved to the town with the smoke and the cars and the people and the identical rows of redbrick houses and the oppressive gray skies, but I barely remember that, and that's not why I'm mad.

I'm taken down a dim, strip-lit corridor, with numbered doors on either side. Some of the doors are brightly decorated with posters of names and KEEP OUT signs. We stop outside the door with the number 4 on it and a viewing slat above it. Inside is a bed with pale-green blankets, a scratchy navy carpet, bare walls, a wardrobe, and a chair. It's white-washed, with one lime-green wall. Who chooses lime green? A whiteboard above the bed and pens in primary colors. Maybe they think I'll write out everything that happened. I imagine it in bloodred, a headstone looming over my pillow.

Two more blue nurses watch me strip to my underwear and scan my body with metal detectors and no regard for dignity. They press stodgy fingers into the lining of my bra and sit on my bed to shake out the contents of my bag into metal trays. I think I can call it my bed, anyway. You aren't allowed pens. Too sharp. You aren't allowed makeup or perfume or drawstrings on trousers or laces on shoes. I can see them glancing at my arms: shiny, raw layers of scar tissue over scar tissue and a few wet cuts. They leave me half a bagful of shitty magazines and one rogue cigarette filter.

I get into bed in my underwear. One of the nurses sits in the open doorway reading a magazine. One-to-one—it's a nice term for suicide watch. I'm not going to be left alone.

I stare at the red light on the ceiling and listen to the nurse turning pages.

I can't get comfortable on the slippery sheets. The curtains, held up by magnets, flutter even though there's no breeze, and the green light from the corridor keeps me forgetting I am in a hospital. Nurses beep in and out of the office next door with a swipe of cards. Distant humming from the motorway. Sirens. Coughing from the nurse in the doorway. Cups of tea coming and going. Envelopes being opened. Whispered conversations.

Rain starts to scratch at the window, and Iris is everywhere. I can see her in the fluttering of the curtains. I can hear her in the rain, and when I close my eyes I can feel her breath on my neck, her arms on my back, her hands around my throat. Her fingernails digging into the palms of my hands. I stumble out of bed with Iris clinging to my ankles, and the nurse gives me two oval sleeping pills. Then I manage to get rid of Iris, until the storm is over and tomorrow begins.

I wake to sharp light. A new nurse is sitting on the chair facing me.

She's short and plump, with dyed dark-red hair that has a sort of mercilessly straightened quality about it. For a while I watch her, still lying in the cocoon I have made for myself, as she flicks quietly through "My husband ate our baby!" in bubble writing. On the floor next to her is a clipboard and an observation sheet.

I sit up. She turns to me.

"Morning," she says brightly. Too brightly. "I'm Emma." She has a faint accent, Scottish, it might be.

I smile awkwardly. That's a thing about me: I'm awkward, I think. I always feel like everything I'm doing is awkward. Even that sentence was awkward.

OK, so there's Emma sitting on one of the standard National Health Service chairs with holes in it and spongy stuffing spewing out, and I'm sitting on my bed and then she asks if I want a shower.

"Yeah," I reply lamely. I say it like I'm struggling to make a decision, even though I've been certain that I want a shower since before I got here. Emphasis on the *y* in "yeah." Why did I do that? I don't know.

"You'll need something to cover your dressings, they can't get wet. We've got some waterproof sleeves you can use . . ." She turns to the wardrobe behind her and passes me a piece of plastic that smells of rubber.

I leave my room and head toward the sign for the nearest bathroom.

"Oh, no, you can't use that one," Emma calls after me. "The cold water doesn't work. It's a safety risk, you might get burned. Don't try the one opposite, either, the shower doesn't work at all in that one."

I follow Emma to a shower room at the other end of the corridor. "This is the only one that works at the moment, sorry!" She giggles.

"OK, thanks."

Emma hovers. Great. She's not leaving.

"Just imagine I'm not here," Emma says, stepping into the bathroom after me. "I've seen it all before."

I start to undress, half clutching the napkin-sized NHS towel against myself, half battling to take off my undershirt with one hand. How can I imagine she isn't there? She *is* there—right there, pretending not to look at my naked body as I fumble with the shower switch, but I know she is looking. You never know, I might try to drown myself in the toilet bowl. I suppose she has to keep her guard up.

The shower shudders unenthusiastically into life. I reach for the curtain.

"Sorry, you're not allowed to shut those."

I turn toward the wall in a last-ditch attempt to preserve my dwindling dignity. I feel every inch of my body as I move under the stuttering shower. I can feel each drop as it splashes against me. My nerves have come alive, and they're fuzzing at each touch. I look down just to check that I'm not sending off electricity sparks. Of course I'm not. Why would I be? Why did I think that?

There are no proper taps in the bathroom, just buttons embedded into the side of the sink. There's no toilet seat, either. I don't know why. They've overestimated my ability to self-destruct. I wouldn't have done anything with a toilet seat, I don't think.

I half-heartedly clean myself with a bar of stodgy soap, not daring to turn around and look at Emma, in case she is laughing at how vile my body is. I don't want to see. The shower shuts off as shampoo is running down my face, and with my eyes closed I search for the switch, splattering against parts of the wall with soapy hands before finding it. If Emma wasn't laughing before, she definitely will be now. Foams of shampoo slide over my shoulders and swirl away into the drains. I blink water out of my eyes and turn the shower off. Cold post-shower air blasts me and I seek warmth from the pathetic towel, but it is no better at that than it was at hiding me from Emma. I pull off the plastic sleeve and there are beads of condensation on my arm. A nurse walks past the open bathroom door, keys jangling from his hips. Nurse? Jailer, more like.

I dress too quickly, shoving on my clothes; the zipper on my jeans scratches against my thigh as I pull them up. Someone calls a patient for their medication.

"I'm asleep," comes the reply from a boy, in a hassled tone. "I'll take them later."

Back down the corridor in Emma's shadow, past a door with a sign that says CLINIC ROOM. Outside is a short queue, two boys and a girl wearing an over-washed Mickey Mouse onesie with the hood up. A nurse hands out paper cups. She watches each patient as they swallow the contents, makes them open their mouths and stick their tongues out afterward. One by one.

Emma keeps up a steady stream of jovial chatter about her three dogs, who aren't allowed on the sofas, the apple tree in her garden, her university friends who don't drink alcohol, the attractive painter redecorating her house . . . I smile and nod and pretend I don't want to be dead.

We end up in a kind of lounge. My damp hair drips down my back. Another nurse in blue sits in a beanbag chair in the corner of the room, his eyes fixed on a TV morning chat show. The flat-screen TV is behind a see-through panel. He's singing "Don't Worry, Be Happy" and raises a hand in my general direction. I quietly sit down on the edge of the nearest sofa, the smallest one, trying to ignore the anxiety that is starting in my stomach and making its way up to my chest and down to my legs and ankles and feet. Pins and needles in my calves. Emma sits next to me.

"Nurse Will, that agency nurse is refusing to give me any acetaminophen because she says Dr. Flores hasn't written it up." The girl in the Mickey Mouse onesie marches into the room.

"And what do you want me to do about it, Alice?" the nurse named Will sings from his beanbag chair.

"I've got a splitting headache . . . Please?" says Alice.

"Can't do anything, sorry," he sings unsympathetically. "Talk to Dr. Flores when he gets in."

"Fine, then," she says grumpily, before sweeping out of the room as dramatically as she came in, apparently not noticing my pathetic presence. Regret is rushing through my veins about every single bloody stupid mistake I've ever made, because now I've ended up here. I can't be here.

"We usually go down for breakfast at eight," says Emma, in an obvious attempt to engage me in conversation.

My mind doesn't have space for mundane things like that. I can't stay here, being followed around like a naughty dog, prodded with metal detectors and viewed through a viewing slat like a different animal, an animal in a zoo. I'm not supposed to be here. I just nod and pretend to look at the clock on the wall, though in truth I can't actually work out what time it is at all, because my brain is too tired and aching from lack of sleep and too much thinking. I read four thirty, which is obviously wrong.

By the time I read quarter to five, more patients are congregating.

"Alice, come over and introduce yourself," says Emma patronizingly to the onesie girl.

"Hi." Alice sits obligingly next to me on the sofa.

"This is Tamar."

"I'm Tamar," I repeat dumbly. How long have I known Alice for? Approximately seven seconds, and I've already made an idiot of myself.

"That's a nice name," she says.

"Thanks."

The conversation dries up. She smiles again and turns to picking her fingernails. Even her fingernails are more interesting than me.

A nurse with lopsided eyeliner appears at the lounge door.

She looks like she's learned to do her makeup on YouTube. "Let's go downstairs," she says. "Breakfast's ready."

The dining room is divided in two. Half of it is made up of blue plastic tables; the other half houses a battered pool table and a sad selection of burgundy chairs. The tables have names, Emma tells me—Ruby, Sapphire, Emerald, Diamond. We are jewels. I sit where I'm told to—at Ruby; that's for people who need more "support," she says—and wait for other people to start eating first. I watch how much they eat and how fast they eat it, and I chew each piece of toast in my mouth twenty times accordingly. There are twelve patients and six nurses.

A boy sits next to me, swaddled in an oversized Batman T-shirt. He looks tired—not in the red-puffy-eyes way; more in his labored movements, the way his limbs seem too heavy for his body and his chin leans low against his neck, as if it is too much effort to hold it up. His lips are dry and a network of small fissures runs through them, as if he doesn't drink enough water, which maybe he doesn't. Maybe he just sticks to the cup of apple juice that he's pouring unsteadily. His hands are a patchwork of scabby grazes, over the knuckles and up to where his fingernails begin, dark and cracked. He spreads butter on his toast but doesn't eat it. Instead he has two cups of clear golden apple juice and a packet of jam that he eats with a teaspoon.

Alice sits opposite me, chewing toast. She's chopped one slice into eight pieces.

On the other side of her is a girl who is curved into herself like a frightened caterpillar. She's holding a piece of paper, crinkled from too much paint. I make out "Harper." Is that her name? It doesn't suit her. Harps are big and clunky and impossible to move but she would be small even if she hadn't starved herself down to nothingness. Her hollow cheekbones mean her glasses perch uncomfortably on her face, making her eyes look huge, like an insect, a bluebottle. She touches the spoon beside her and flinches. Spoons don't bite.

Nurse Will and Lopsided Nurse eat their breakfasts at our table, too, acting as though they aren't interested in how much we eat, what we eat, or how we eat it. It's not convincing. That's why they're there. As soon as they finish one plate of food, something else is produced: cereal, yogurt, juice. Alice eats it all solemnly and pensively. Except for the milk.

"I'm not drinking it," says Alice flatly. "It's disgusting."

"You've got to drink it," says Nurse Will. "Just chug it all down in one gulp and it'll be over before you know it."

I scrape Flora over my toast, listening to the argument as it brews at the Ruby table.

"Two sugars are the way to do it," Emma says, ripping open packets of sugar and pouring them into her mug. "There's no other way as far as I'm concerned."

"I've had milk on my cereal already this morning, I'm not drinking it as well," Alice says adamantly.

"Look, Alice, we're not having this discussion again," says Agency Nurse from a chair across the room. "You need to drink the milk."

"I'm not fucking drinking it!" she shouts suddenly, swiping her arm across the table, slapping the cup to the floor. She stands up in one swift movement of panic.

"Could you just pass the milk?" says Emma to the boy in the Batman T-shirt, apparently not noticing the irony. She stirs it into her tea.

"Sit down, Alice," says Nurse Will, standing up as well.

"No," she says, climbing away from the table and making for the door, but Lopsided Nurse is there before her, holding it shut.

"Get out of the way!" screams Alice. "You can't make me drink it, fuck off!"

"Don't swear at me" is all Lopsided Nurse says.

The boy continues to scrape out jam from the corners of the packet as if this scene is perfectly normal. I hope it isn't perfectly normal, but I can't help but worry that it probably is. I try to concentrate on my toast but it's impossible. Alice is screaming and fighting her way to the door handle as Nurse Will tries to grab her.

"Get off me! Go away!"

"Calm down, Alice," says Nurse Will, grappling to keep her arms together behind her back. "Calm down."

"Fuck you, and your stupid fucking milk!"

No point crying over spilled milk, I think. It lies in a puddle on the floor.

I can't be here. What am I doing here?

Most of the patients disappear to Therapy Room 1 for a vaguely named "education session," but I'm not allowed. I sit on a burgundy chair until Alice is brought back in—she's quieter now. A boy appears suddenly and sits on the chair next to me without so much as a glance in my direction. He is holding knitting needles and wool.

"Where were you at breakfast?" I ask after a while. I hadn't seen him that morning.

"In bed," he says. "I'm a serial cereal avoider." He probably spent the extra hour in bed thinking up that pun.

He starts knitting aggressively, with elaborate arm movements and nimble fingers; maybe he's done too much knitting, been locked away for too long. He's pale, so pale and thin that wiry blue veins branch down his translucent arms and the bones in his elbows jut out in unnatural directions. His dark hair falls messily against his head. It's almost black, an eerie contrast to his ivory skin. I watch his emaciated legs jigging in his blue polyester tracksuit. His gray eyes are focused on the knitting with an almost obsessive glare. I'm not sure if I like him.

"Jasper's notorious," cuts in Alice from the other side of the lounge. "They wake him up at six o'clock but he still manages to miss it." There's a note of bitterness in her voice. I guess she wants to miss breakfast, too.

"I don't eat cereal," Jasper continues airily. "I don't agree with it."

"Jasper also doesn't agree with cotton candy, for the record. He says it's like eating a flavored wig. Reminds him of his grandma. Nothing at all to do with the sugar content," she adds snarkily.

"If you'd seen my grandma's hair, you'd hate cotton candy as well!" He makes a gagging noise.

"You're an idiot," says Alice. "Anyway, Tamar, I mean, do we have to call you that? Do you not have a nickname?"

"What's wrong with her name?" snaps Jasper. "I'm sorry my friend is being so rude," he adds to me. He's being sarcastic, I think.

"You can call me Tay. Tay, Tamar, whatever. I don't mind."

"Cool, so, Tay, have you met everyone?" says Alice. "Patient Will—the guy who ate jam for breakfast—has been here the longest out of all of us, coming up on a year. He's lovely but sometimes he doesn't take things as a joke."

"He's psychotic," Jasper offers helpfully. "He was in a right state when they swapped his meds a few weeks ago, banging on about God knows what at God knows what time of the night."

"Louis," Alice chimes in. "Everyone loves Louis."

"Nothing more to say about Louis, really," says Jasper. "You missed him—he used to have your room. Left a few days ago. He's so normal he makes everyone else look even crazier than we already are."

"Except he was paralyzed in his left leg," says Alice. "He had this thing where his emotional stress manifested itself physically, so actually he wasn't really paralyzed at all. Can't remember what it's called. Weird, I know."

"Alice," says the Lopsided Nurse warningly.

"Then that just leaves us, I guess," says Jasper, turning to Alice.

"The eating disorders," Alice says, raising her hands in a thumbs-up. "Three of us were discharged earlier this week, so now there's only three of us, but Harper doesn't speak, so I guess she doesn't count."

"So, why're you here?" Jasper says, turning back to me.

"I—"

"No, don't tell us! We have to guess."

"You're on one-to-one, which means you're obviously really dangerous . . ." Alice starts. "I reckon you're paranoid.

You couldn't find the meaning of life so you compensated with drugs until you got so high you ended up in the back of a police car on a one-way trip to the funny farm."

"Bullshit," says Jasper. "She's not paranoid, are you, Tamar? I'm thinking desperately insecure but disguised as a psychopath."

Charming.

But they're right. It's my fault that Iris is dead so, yes, I'm a psychopath.

Lopsided Nurse shifts uncomfortably in her chair. She opens her mouth as if to say something, her lower jaw hovering for a few seconds, before shutting it and returning her attention to her magazine.

"So . . . ? Who's closer?"

"Oh, I just . . ." Where do I start? Why am I here? I'm here because I'm a murderer. *Hi, I'm Tamar, and I am a murderer. Nice to meet you.* Is that what they want to hear, though?

"I had a breakdown, I guess. I . . . tried to kill myself."

"Join the club," says Alice, reaching out to shake my

hand as if it's something to be proud of. "What did you do?"

The nurse looks up again. "I'm not sure this is a suitable conversation to be having, Alice. How about you change the topic?"

Alice rolls her eyes. "Fine, then. It's weird, isn't it? That a mental hospital is the one place you can't talk about stuff like this. They banned us from playing hangman as well," she adds, before standing up and wandering out of the room.

Jasper jiggles his legs up and down.

"Stop it, Jasper," says Lopsided Nurse.

"Stop what?" he says in false indignation, but his legs do stop. "How long do I have left?"

"Fifteen minutes, then you can go."

"For God's sake." He picks up the half-knitted scarf. "Whose is this, anyway?" He starts to knit without waiting for an answer. His legs begin to shake again.

"What're the rules about smoking?" I say suddenly, realizing that the restless feeling that I have is because I haven't had a cigarette for days. I hadn't remembered to. Am I even a smoker?

"Not allowed," says Jasper. "Don't even bother asking any of the nurses on shift today. They'll all say no. Good thing is, they change so often, you probably won't see half of them again, so you can just ask the next batch tonight. Sometimes you get lucky."

I wonder if I'm expected to get up and do something. Not that there's anything to do, or anywhere to go. Milk remains spilled on the wooden floor, a tribute to Alice's angry refusal at breakfast. They just replaced it with more milk, so she ended up having to drink some anyway.

Jasper continues to jiggle his legs and knit.

THEN

That night, the one after the dam, Iris's mum rang my dad and they spoke for quite some time. I'm not sure exactly what was said. Afterward my dad came into my bedroom and sat on the end of my polka-dot duvet cover.

I was pretending to be enthralled by my biology textbook. I still felt drunk from the afternoon.

"Tamar, I've just been on the phone with Iris's mum. She's very worried because Iris hasn't come home yet. Did she tell you if she was going anywhere? She couldn't have left with someone else?"

"No," I said, looking up, "she said she was getting the bus at eight fifteen. When I left her it was only ten minutes until it was due to arrive. I don't know where she would be if she didn't catch it. I don't know, sorry, I'll text her."

So I wrote a text to Iris. I sent three kisses and asked her if she was all right.

Later that night my dad came into my room again and asked if I was OK—it wasn't like me to spend so much time up here, alone. I replied that I was fine, thank-you-very-much. He left again, but came back a few minutes later with a chipped mug of tea. Tea—the cure for all.

"Have you heard back from her?" He faltered as I shook my head. "Iris's mum thinks it might be time to get the police involved."

"Wha—?" I spluttered, color rushing to my face like I had been turned upside down. "The police? But she's not, I mean, you don't think . . ."

Dad never got rattled by anything. He kissed me on the forehead, got up, and left, and I did not see him for the rest of the night.

I thought the police would come immediately, sniff out the guilt lurking beneath my lowered eyes, handcuff me and whisk me off to prison because I was *evil*. But they didn't. They didn't come until late afternoon the next day—a man and a woman with a blonde bob. Dad talked to them first, offered them cups of tea. They declined, I remember. They wanted water instead. I sat at the bottom of the stairs, listening to the quiet murmurs behind the half-open living room door, watching the clock in the hall shudder with each passing second. The dull hangover in my head thumped.

Less than twenty-four hours ago, we were drinking by the dam.

Our living room was different back then from how it looks now. We still had the cream leather sofa that we'd had since

I was a baby. My parents went through a phase when most things were leather. Easier for wiping up baby puke, I suppose. The floor was pale and wooden, but no one bothered to polish it, so if you walked with bare feet you ended up with a splinter or three. There was a collection of small china animals on the mantelpiece, too: a ginger cat curled up next to the candle holders, a seal, a tawny owl with a broken beak, family photos.

The policewoman was named Kerri, I think. I'm not sure how she spelled it, though; there are lots of ways you can spell Kerri. She called me "darling" a lot and phrased her questions like they were meant for a four-year-old. The first thing that they wanted to make clear to me was that I wasn't in any trouble. *You're not in any trouble.* Ha. They were just here to ask some questions, and perhaps I could help them. It wouldn't take long.

"Tamar, I want you to imagine for a minute that you are Iris. Where might you have gone? Who are you closest to?"

Policeman Philip, I think he was named, said, "Maybe one of your school friends?" Philip had tattoos covering his arms and up his neck to where it met the stubble below his chin. It looked hard, until you realized it was just fish and a dolphin.

"I don't know," I said. "She said she was getting the bus, that's all she said. I left because she said she was leaving soon, otherwise I would've waited with her. I should've waited with her, I'm sorry."

"You don't need to be sorry, darling. Was Iris drunk?"

"A bit, yeah. I mean, she could still walk."

"She could still walk? Could she walk easily?"

"She was a bit unsteady, we both were. I really don't remember, I'm so shocked."

"We understand, darling."

Actually, they didn't understand. They didn't understand that the shock was because I was now a murderer, laced with bloodthirsty evil like Jack the Ripper. I wasn't shocked for Iris. I was shocked for me. The police carried on asking me questions, and I carried on responding. After a while they left, their glasses of water untouched on the sideboard. They were sure she'd turn up, they told me. I shouldn't worry.

They found Iris's body half a mile down the river, at the place where it starts to meander around the city outskirts. It was black and oil tinted, tossed up in the stinking mudbanks among broken beer bottles and deflated children's balloons. The charcoal shadows of sprawling warehouses hung low over the murky water. She was battered and bruised, swollen, her auburn hair entangled in overhanging branches. Seagulls had already begun to pick at her, squawking and bickering over her corpse. In fact, that was how they found her: from the unexplained mob of white, swooping birds.

It's not your fault, Tamar.
Dwelling on it won't help.
Iris made bad decisions.
You're not responsible.
It was an accident.
You're not in trouble.

NOW

Time moves differently in a psychiatric hospital. So differently, in fact, that it sometimes can seem as if time has stopped altogether. The tears roll oh-so-slowly. The days fuse together, swallowed into the whitewashed walls and plates of frozen dinners and risperidone. I watch daytime TV for what-must-be-an-hour, only to see the second hand triumphantly meeting the twelve: It's been only a minute. Turn to the TV. Repeat. Someone kicks off and gets restrained. Mood is ruined. At least it's not me. Turn back to the TV. Eat. There's only so much Jeremy Kyle you can watch. Repeat. Is the clock ticktocking? Watch post-watershed TV for, let's see, six rounds of the second hand, before Emma says turn it off because it's "inappropriate." Try to sleep. Fail to sleep. Go back to the lounge and the TV and change the channel to something less inappropriate. End up watching Alice arguing with the nurses about broken showers for the third time today. Harper paints her nails with fierce concentration. Play one round of Trivial Pursuit with Patient Will until his meds kick in and his eyes glaze over. He knows the answer to every single question. The nurses' station beeps. Something chugs out of the printer in the corner. Maybe notes about that evil new patient on the block, Tamar. Clock hits 10 p.m. I go back to bed. I'm off one-to-one now—that's something.

Dr. Flores hasn't given up trying to make me talk. He tries to catch me when I'm not expecting him—early in the morning before breakfast, when I haven't even brushed my teeth.

"So, let's have a thought shower about some possible triggers for the self-harm."

"Thought shower?"

Dr. Flores is an idiot.

"Yes," he says, as if it should be obvious. "Like a brainstorm, except we don't use that phrase anymore."

I roll my eyes.

"Can you stop?" Dr. Flores raises one eyebrow. He's good at doing that. I used to try when I was younger, contorting my face in front of the mirror, but I never managed it.

"I've tried before and I can't do it," I say. "I feel even worse."

"You can do it," he insists. "It's like any addiction, Tamar. You can, it's just that it's very difficult. I've seen people do it."

"Why do you think people die from addictions, then?" I snap. I watch him switch on his pondering face. I don't think he's ever really pondering; he just wants to make it look as though everything that comes out of his mouth is carefully constructed gold.

"Because not everyone wants to get better. Do you want to get better, Tamar?"

Do I want to get better? That, I guess, is the big question, the question that will answer every single problem in the land. Do I want to get better? Dr. Flores stares at me for ten seconds.

"I don't know," I mumble. Shouldn't I know? I should know. The answer should be obvious. I'm supposed to want to get better. "I don't want to feel like this anymore."

"Do you want to get better?" he repeats. "There's a difference between wanting to get better and *wanting* to get better. I think everyone can recover. It takes time—it might take years, but it can be done."

He's talking generally; he's not saying "you." Why? Am I the exception to the otherwise flawless rule?

"Don't you talk to anyone at all? How about your friends at school?"

I laugh. "What friends?"

I did have friends, once.

I'd known Toby since I was four, and Mia since primary

school, and ever since year nine we'd followed the same morning ritual: two cigarettes each between the yellow lines in the pedestrian-only area at eight in the morning, before the school buses arrived half an hour later. A few eager year sevens with oversized backpacks struggled up the school drive, their skinny frames heaving under the weight of soon-to-be-forgotten cellos and sports uniforms. It was normal, because Toby had his shirt hanging out like he always did, and Mia's hair was French-braided and hung on her left side like it always did. The dark concrete school buildings stood behind us, a jigsaw of gray teaching blocks sitting between a network of colored walkways. It probably looked better from above.

People began to back away when I went insane; it didn't take them long to catch on. Tamar: the strange loner freak with scars on her thighs and cobwebs in her moldy gray-blue brain. "Keep away from Tamar," parents warned their children. "She's trouble, that girl." My illness didn't command sympathy and grapes and bunches of flowers. No sympathy for psychos. People didn't want to have anything to do with that girl, the one who sliced her own skin for fun. But I wasn't trouble; I was *in* trouble.

"I haven't had friends for a long time," I say, and Dr. Flores laughs, even though I'm not joking.

"Don't be melodramatic—I'm sure you have some friends. Who did you sit next to at school?"

"The wall," I say.

"What about Toby, then? He's your friend?"

"Sometimes, I guess, yeah."

My first memory of Toby was when we were both four, at a garden party hosted by his parents. Barbecue grills were smoking pink prawns that oozed pale oil, and I'd had my hand slapped by my dad for trying to pick one off and almost scalding my fingers raw. Toby had taken me to the garden shed because we were going to play hide-and-seek, and I was the seeker. He told me to wait in there, count for twenty seconds. It was cold and damp, and a fat black spider spun a web above my head with nimble, hairy legs. I stood up close against the rusty children's bikes and broken deck chairs, picking clumps of cobweb out of my ponytail. I counted to thirteen, then waited a few more seconds because I'd gotten confused and didn't make it to twenty. I could hear the clinking of glasses two meters away under the bare cherry tree. The door was locked. My dad found me squatting in the corner next to the old rabbit hutch and the sawdust it had spilled, crying and crying like the world was over. Toby had to apologize to me and a few days later I received a card that he'd obviously been forced to draw, of him and me holding hands.

"Do your friendships make you think about self-harming?" Dr. Flores says.

"More like the lack of friends."

"Ah." Dr. Flores scribbles on his pad.

"But it's more complicated than that," I say. He raises his eyebrows.

"And that's why you're here," he says. "OK, so, friends aside, what else are we thinking about the self-harm?"

He's a great one for collaborative pronouns, the ones that say we're all in this together, one big, dysfunctional, suicidal team. Except we're not. At five o'clock each day

Dr. Flores and the nurses can trot home to their families and watch TV and forget about all the shit that they have heard during the day. The shit stops at the end of each shift.

I tell him the self-harm's going swimmingly, thank-you-very-much.

"But what does it do for you? In the moment? Does it feel good?"

Now it's my turn to laugh. "I'm slicing my own skin. Of course it doesn't feel good," I say. "It feels horrible. That's kind of the point."

"I see," Dr. Flores says. He's the one who should be telling me. He knows all about the blades-on-skin-equals-endorphins-rushing thing. He told me about it in the first place. "Why do it, then?"

Is he accusing me of something? I shrug, as if I'm pondering something. I'm not. My brain is blank.

"Well, it's a feeling," I say. "It's better than feeling nothing at all. At least it's something."

Dr. Flores doesn't agree. He bites his pen. "Do you feel numb? Or empty?" He wants me to say yes, because he'd be one step closer to matching me up with the jargon in his diagnostic manual. I don't play ball.

"No."

"I'm going to raise your medication. It'll make you sleepy."

"I know."

"How are you feeling?" (On a scale of one to ten—he doesn't have to say it.)

"Eleven."

"Good." He doesn't have time for my sarcasm. "Do you want to leave?"

"Always."

He smiles.

If you hit your head against the hardest surface you can find, the bad thoughts shake around your skull so long that they take time to recompose themselves. It's like when a bus stops suddenly and your groceries go everywhere, so you have to rummage around the legs of strangers, wishing you hadn't bought quite such a large quantity of rice now that the bag has split open. You can actually feel the thoughts cracking against the bone. The hardest surface in a psychiatric hospital is the bedroom wall. If you slam your forehead hard enough, then it bleeds under the skin and the bruises are swollen and sore, but at least the thoughts disappear for a third of a second. Bam. A moment of emptiness. Bam. A moment of serenity and calm and quiet.

Problem is, once the dizziness starts to dissipate, the bad thoughts shout again in a second wind of anger and intensity because now not only are you pathetic and fat and ugly, you're also a stupid little git for thinking banging your head against a wall was going to get rid of them. So, before you know it, your head is cracking against the wall again with a resounding thump, so it's a bit of a vicious circle, really.

Bam.

What perfect logic.

Emma doesn't think it's perfect logic, and she asks me what the hell I was doing as she hands me an ice pack she's brought up from the kitchen freezer.

"What are you trying to do, break a hole in the wall?" She tells me I'll have to pay for it to be repaired. "You don't have to do that, you know, you can just come and talk to one of us."

"You were all busy," I say, pressing the ice pack against my aching head.

"I'm sure we could have made time," she responds. "We can all hear you from the nurses' office anyway."

I'm not sure that they could or would have made time, but I say nothing. People only make time for you when things get dramatic. That's been my experience, anyway.

"Do you want to talk about anything now?"

"No," I say. Emma can't even hide her irritation and desire to be doing anything else; I don't want to bother her.

"It's better to talk than to do that to your head, you know."

"My head's already fucked up," I snap at her.

"It isn't, but don't make things worse for yourself, Tamar. You're supposed to be going out with your mum tomorrow."

Don't care don't care.

She passes me risperidone in a paper cup. If you pull all the folds out, then flatten them, they go from paper cup to perfectly round paper plate. I have a collection on my bedside table.

Ice pressing down. Melting drips of water from my forehead onto my rough lips. A lump in my throat because I didn't use enough water to swallow and the risperidone has lingered. The clock on the wall hits ten, which means it is now an acceptable time to crawl into bed and hide.

"You're not going to put me back on one-to-one, are you?" I ask Emma as she tidies away blankets strewn on the floor.

"No," she says. "We'll raise it to fifteen-minute obs, though. I'll tell the rest of the team."

"OK," I say, relieved. I don't fancy the idea of more nights trying not to notice someone staring at me through the gloom.

I hobble to bed and curl under the covers, still in the clothes I've worn all day. I can't be bothered to change. I close my eyes.

Fifteen minutes later, a torch flashes into my face and I start like a deer in headlights.

"Just doing checks," hisses Emma. "Sorry."

I turn over so I'm facing away from the door. You don't get used to stuff like that. The risperidone kicks in.

The world feels different after you've left it for a while. Bolder colors, brighter lights, bigger engines in bigger cars. Louder.

I notice the dents in the newly spread tarmac on the road, the way the traffic lights flicker before turning yellow, the magnified sound a crisp packet makes when crushed underfoot. I notice the lumpy shapes that chewing gum makes on the pavement, and the different shades of brown on bark. A man hurries past in a suit that is just lighter than navy, and I notice there's a button missing on his jacket, second from the top. The greasy smell of KFC. The sound of needles whirring in a tattoo studio.

Mum holds my hand, and I squeeze hers back as we walk down the main road from Lime Grove. We're OK, I think.

We go to the closest shopping center and wander without talking around the glass-domed halls, listening to the echoes of a busker's guitar. A stall is still selling roasted chestnuts, even though Christmas is long gone, and the burnt smell hovers in the air. The escalators are broken, and they're blocked at each entrance by red-and-white tape, as if stationary escalators are somehow far more dangerous than the ones that run away when you step on them.

I should be happy to be out and clutching hands with my mum, with no alarms going off or threats of needles shoved into uncomfortable places if you don't do as you're told. But

I'm not. I'm overwhelmed and frightened and the wings of bad thoughts have started to flutter again in the clouds of my brain.

Ignore them.

I pull on my mask of happy and OK; I have to. My mum is tired, but she smiles at me, and she's happier than I've seen her in months and months. She insists on buying me two sudoku books from WHSmith, because, she says, I need to keep my mind occupied, and apparently sudokus are the way to do that.

"How's Dad?" I ask.

"Lunch?" she replies instead, dragging me toward the nearest café.

My dad works in a bathroom showroom. He can swap from smooth, slick, suited-and-booted to football-watching, beer-guzzling, and rough-edged in the space of seconds, as soon as he comes through the door, takes his tie off, and hooks it on the coat hanger. He hasn't been to see me at Lime Grove. I don't think he can. I don't blame him.

When I was little, he wore his hair down to his shoulders

with braids and velvet hair bands, had incorrect Latin quotes on his forearms, and played the guitar. Mum's different now, too. She used to wear golden hoop earrings and patchwork quilts fashioned into jackets. We lived on the small red barge then. Mum kept an herb garden in fawn terra-cotta pots on the roof: thyme, mint, coriander. I used to go fishing in adjacent streams with my puppy, Brew, my trousers rolled up to my knees, scooping a bucket into the marbled water and watching minnows the size of my fingers dart away into the lily pads. I always let them go. I just wanted to look.

Mum orders a toasted sandwich for me now, and as I wrestle with the strings of melted cheese stretching from the bread onto my chin she swirls the foam heart on her macchiato into shapelessness. My mum never eats much. She's tall and thin and has been on almost every fad diet that there is, as they come and go. Rubbery mozzarella sticks in between my teeth and against my gums, but I can taste it; the tomatoes are fresh and juicy and they burst against my tongue. I think about the half-frozen plate of regurgitated cat food I battled my way through for dinner last night.

Being out feels stranger and stranger; no one looks at me as if I'm going to hurt them or hurt myself. People don't do a double take as I go into the toilet, as if to ask: *What are you doing? Why are you going there?*

What? Are? Your? Intentions?

They trust that I am safe to go to the toilet on my own. What a treat.

The clock eats away at the hour we have left together. I flick through the pages of Waterstones's bestsellers—tales of drug abuse and families torn apart by war, as if we need more terrible things to think about. New books have a strange smell to them. I can't put my finger on what it is, but I like it. It's comforting.

"Superdrug?" says Mum eventually as I study a book about hieroglyphics with mild interest. "You can stock up on things. Body wash, tampons, you know. Hairpins? Might be good if you're not washing your hair." Showers in Lime Grove are so heavily rationed that "self-neglect" has become a normal part of our abnormal lives. "The shampoos are three for two," she goes on. "Come and choose which one you want, because they all smell the same to me."

I choose peach and papaya, lime and mint, and bubble-gum scents, put them into her basket.

"Ooh, nail polish!" She beams. She couldn't be happier that her daughter is out in the real world for a few fleeting hours. "They've got silver . . . That would suit you. It would go with your hair," she says, picking up two bottles with a smile and dropping them into the basket with a clink. She squeezes my arm and turns to the till.

Cuts flinch under the jumper, under her touch.

The shift from OK to not OK is so quick and so dramatic that, all at once, I know what Dr. Flores meant when he said I was unpredictable, volatile.

I focus on the stacks of hair dyes—Raspberry Rebel, Cosmic Blue—and beauty products—face wash, face wipes, razor blades . . .

I can feel the shift in my body, a surge of warped energy boiling up as my mood crashes into the abyss. It is a physical change. I can barely stop my fingers from shaking as I fumble open the nearest packet, pry out the razors with trembling fingers that don't belong to me—I'm not doing it—shove them deep into the crevasses of my jacket pocket. A familiar itch is creeping up my arms. It is time to move on. It's too late to move on. The shift has already occurred.

While she is paying, I stumble to the shop's baby-changing bathroom, adrenaline still swelling my veins, sit down on the hard toilet seat (it has a seat—how unusual), and hold my head in between my trembling legs.

It takes me twenty seconds to extract the blades from the razor with a 5p coin. I snap open the pack of hairpins, curl my hair into a bun, slip the blades into it, held in by a hairpin. You can't see them. They're covered by wispy locks of greasy hair the color of a faded pink orchid.

I gather my thoughts into a bundle in my arms.

I'm not OK anymore. I'm not OK.

But it doesn't matter. Because I have three strips of cold metal entwined in my hair.

"New patient alert!" shouts Jasper suddenly, jumping up from the Ruby table and conveniently spilling his apple juice on the floor as he does so.

We're halfway through dinnertime on the day after my leave and Harper has been crying so much over her baked potato that her glasses have steamed.

"Not this again," Nurse Will mutters as everyone clanks down their cutlery and dashes to the window.

Jasper climbs up onto the windowsill and slaps his hands against the pane, his fingerprints clouding the glass. He and Alice stick their tongues out, contorting their faces and making weird noises.

"Jasper, Alice, get back to the table. All of you, in fact, get back to your seats. Leave them alone, you'll see them soon enough." Agency Nurse claps her hands sharply together and they head back to their seats, chortling as if nothing has ever been so hilarious.

"What the hell was that about?" I say to Alice as she non-chalantly picks up her fork.

"We were just giving our new patient a mental-hospital welcome," she says. "You know, lunatic style."

I look out the window. The new patient in question is stumbling out of a police car clutching a plastic bag of possessions and nothing else. Black mark. No plastic bags allowed here. A policeman watches her warningly and ushers her toward the front door ahead of him. She has dark ginger hair tousled in a messy clump below her shoulders. Not quite auburn, like Iris's, but red enough to make me squirm.

The front doorbell chimes through the unit three times. The policeman is impatient. He has better things to do than be a taxi service for teenage girls. I bet that's what he's thinking. Agency Nurse pours another two hundred milliliters of apple juice up to the line but no farther and slides it across the table to Jasper, who shakes his head but drinks it anyway, in one long gulp, like he's taking pills. Alice drinks hers in minuscule sips between each tiny mouthful of bland potato. Different techniques, same calories.

The new patient enters the dining room during after-meal sit-down, smiling like she hasn't just been locked up in a mental hospital. She's picked up a nurse, who trails behind her in a flurry of NHS azure. She's welcomed in the same way that I was, with a bagel with smoked salmon that's browning at the edges and a tiny helping of cream cheese.

"I can't eat anything, sorry, I'm too excited," she says, bouncing from foot to foot. She is clearly mistaking anxiety for a positive emotion.

"Why don't you have a seat and introduce yourself?" Agency Nurse says.

"Hi," says the girl, grinning around at our sorry collection of faces. "I'm Elle."

"Barking mad," Jasper whispers to me in between frantic shakes of his leg. "So, Elle, what you in for?"

Elle is radiating too much confidence for a new patient. Her face is so flushed that her hundreds of freckles—on her cheeks and the bridge of her nose—are almost hidden.

"I was at another unit before I came here, in Dorset, but they moved me up here because it's closer to home . . ."

"Oh, isn't that good of them?" cuts in Alice sarcastically.

Elle ignores her. "Well, when I say home, I mean my foster parents' house, so it's not really my home at all."

"I'm sorry," I say awkwardly, but she laughs.

"Don't be. I'm as free as a bird. Better than living at home any day." She doesn't expand, and I don't ask her to.

"How long were you at your last place for?" I say as Alice rolls her eyes and leaves the room, scraping her chair and slamming the door.

"About a month, I think. Maybe less. It was just until another bed opened up. And now it has!" she finishes brightly. Her eyes are very green, and strangely round, like a cat's. They dominate her face somehow. She's pretty, though, in an unconventional way. "What about you?"

"Oh, I've only been here a few weeks—"

"So you're a newbie, then? Welcome!" Elle says, apparently not noticing that I'm less new than her.

"Kind of, yeah," I reply, puzzled by the genuine warmth in her face, as if we've been friends for years. "I didn't think I'd be here even this long, to be honest."

"At my last place, there was a boy who'd been there for nearly four years," says Elle. "He was basically a permanent fixture. Like a tap," she adds thoughtfully.

"Shit. Well, I'm not going to stay here that long," I say.

"How do you know?"

"My psychiatrist said it wouldn't be long," I say, although suddenly I'm starting to doubt this.

Elle laughs. "You believed that? I don't believe a word any of them say. They said they wouldn't section me or make me take medication, and now look at me." She laughs again, but there's a lingering bitterness this time. Without explanation, she stands up, walks to the sofa opposite, and sits down again, tucking the nearest cushion under her chin.

"You're sectioned?" I say, studying her.

"Yeah, since last week. I wasn't taking the meds they gave me."

"So they made you take them?"

"They can't make me do anything. They just think they can," she says with an air of sly delight.

New patients rock the unhappy state of volatile equilibrium we've built for ourselves. Now we'll have to start from the beginning again, incorporating Elle into the brickwork.

"A bit of lamotrigine for the lovely Elle," sings Nurse Will in an unrecognizable tune, "and some more fluoxetine for the fabulous Elle, and a nice piece of risperidone for the ravishing Tamar."

"Stop being so creepy," I say to him as I take the pill from the paper cup he hands to me, like always. It's almost ten o'clock, almost time for bed again.

I watch Elle as she puts her pill in her mouth and swigs

back water. I watch her as she takes the pill back out again and slips it into her pocket with unnerving skill. She doesn't see me looking at her.

"I've got even more fluoxetine for the fantastic Alice!" Nurse Will calls out.

I can still hear him singing, "Quetiapine for the quintessentially curious Will," as I leave the clinic room and walk down the corridor to my bedroom.

"Oh, Will, you super thing, we've also got you some sertraline!"

Hooray. Super lucky pill-guzzling Patient Will. Mental hospitals have an extraordinarily warped view of reality. Which, I guess, is quite ironic, when you think about it.

It takes half an hour for the risperidone to kick in: a huge pressure pounding against my eyelids as my head droops onto the pillow that's still damp from last night's dribble. Risperidone sleep isn't like other sleep; you can sleep for twelve hours but you still won't wake up refreshed and buzzing and ready to face the day. It's not that sort of sleep. I'm vaguely aware of my bedroom door swinging open, the harsh light of a torch flashing against my face, then a click and a return to the darkness. I don't know the time.

However, I do know that at one thirty in the morning, Patient Will kicks off. I recognize his voice now. Listening to someone else having a madness attack is frightening. You want to go and grab them and hold them but hugs don't fix Patient Will, because if I tried to do that, he would think I was strangling him and his frantic breathing would become more and more frenzied and he would probably hit me. I don't leave my room as Patient Will shouts the building down, his labored breaths drumming louder and louder and LOUDER in my head, engulfed in terror and confusion that nothing can solve.

In some ways, it's more frightening when it isn't happening to you, because at least then you can feel every single awful sensation in your body, and you can clutch hold of them and let them wax and wane. I can only hear, and hope that he makes it through the night in no more than two pieces.

Luckily, I'm too dosed up to worry for long. I guess that's why some people call psychiatry "social control." I understand that now. But I'm also too drugged up to protest for change.

THEN

At Iris's funeral, everyone wore purple and yellow, like the flower, but that didn't hide the fact that autumn was sidling in and everything was decaying. It was a dull Monday afternoon, and the gray clouds hung low in sprawling shapes like giant puppets.

Iris's coffin was oblong and pine, unceremoniously draped in a white sheet, like her parents hadn't wanted to think about it. They sat on the front pew in church, eyes fixed straight ahead, arms linked. They didn't cry, but pain was sculpted into the ridges of their brows, into the skin hanging loosely from jutting cheekbones, their un-ironed clothes, the stubble on her father's chin that looked like hundreds of tiny parasites. I watched them. They didn't cry.

The church was small, and the stained-glass window poured a kaleidoscope of light onto the altar. Iris's cousin reminisced in the pulpit about that time when they fell into the wasps' nest and spent the night smothered in vinegar, but no one laughed. *Iris was a gem*, he said.

Outside, the gravestones were small but each one was tended with an unnerving dedication, with perfectly cut grass and jars of red roses.

The air was cool and I could see my breath swirling in front of me. I thought of Mia, how we used to pretend to be dragons when we were younger, snarling and chasing each other in the frosty school playground, until things went wrong.

I felt cold hands clutch my shoulders, and Mia locked me in an awkward embrace. "You all right?" she said.

"Yeah," I replied. I didn't deserve Mia's comfort, didn't want it. "You're holding me too tight. I can't breathe."

Mia loosened her arms. "Sorry, Tay."

I ran out of the creaking church gates, ran all the way to the main road in a numb trance, caught the first bus I found, and did not get off until it terminated at the edge of the city, an hour later. I walked home.

One step, two step.

Let me tell you how anxiety is.

I knew people were looking, because my footsteps were too loud even though I was trying to be quiet. I was painfully aware of myself and I tried to focus on the cracks in the pavement as I walked, because apparently that's the thing to do, but I just ended up swaying sideways and almost crashing into a child. *Oh, God, it looked deliberate. That kid's parent is going to think I'm some kind of psycho trying to beat her son up; quick: apologize, apologize. Now!*

Of course I said nothing and just scuttled awkwardly past like a crab, which was terrible because now that mother was going to hate me forever and ever and I coulddn't rectify the situation. I'd only been out five minutes and I'd already ruined someone's life. What if that kid's mother goes to the police about me? I briefly considered buying a different outfit from the charity shop across the road but I couldn't go in there because I'd never been there before and it might be a front for drugs, kidnapping, or prostitution. So instead I just turned into the corner shop and checked from behind the postcard stand that the person at the registers was someone I knew.

So, I was standing there at the register and Lucy was in an unusually friendly mood. I knew she was doing it to compensate for the fact that she'd noticed the slight wobble in my eyeliner and was trying to act normal so I didn't feel deathly embarrassed. I tried to fix it before the funeral, I really did, but it's hard to do when your hands won't stop trembling. I redid it four times before I went, but it didn't help, as eyeliner is always best the first time around anyway.

She was asking me what A-levels I'm taking and I was looking frantic and going red and trying to speak but it was
coming out in a high-pitched screech like a dying eagle or
something, so instead I just mumbled under my breath
something about the Cold War, which I knew she'd find
desperately boring but I said it anyway because it was better
than the silence. By now Lucy was staring at my every
imperfection and I was painfully awkward; she was looking
at the way I was standing—perhaps my back was too
hunched or my arm looked unnaturally placed? *Oh, God,*
what if I have food in between my teeth? A knot in my
hair? Heavy breathing, ugly legs, weird laugh, horrible
clothes, horrible face, horrible voice, horrible, horrible,
horrible. But Lucy just smiled and said, "History A-level?
Oh, that's nice." She made a joke about Rasputin that
I didn't understand, then I grabbed my cigarettes, bared
my teeth in what was supposed to be a smile, and left.

The bell tinkled as the door shut and I saw a police car
driving down the street. I wanted to cry. *That's it—they're*
looking for me. Heads down, boys. Keep looking at those

cracks. I was counting musical instruments in my head because I couldn't think of anything else and I needed to stay calm.

Piano, cello, oboe.

The police car crawled toward me and I was sure it was slowing down.

Bassoon.

I could feel my heart rate going funny, like a broken clock. No, no, I needed to stay calm. The police car drew up beside me and I continued staring at the cracks in the pavement. Maybe, if I can't see them, they can't see me.

Saxophone. Violin.

The police car drove past and I watched its blue-and-yellow checks become smaller and smaller until it passed through the traffic lights and disappeared at the round-about. I stayed put for a few minutes to allow the dizziness in my head to subside, and then I walked home, trying to ignore the fact that I knew someone was following me.

When I got home, I frantically unlocked the front door and staggered up to my bedroom, panting and shaking like a dog. I smoked half the pack of cigarettes out of my window, curled up into my curtains. It made me feel sick, but I would choose sick over terrified any day.

I am never, ever, for as long as I live, leaving the house again.

NOW

"**Time to learn!**" exclaims Nurse Will. "Education is the building block of success, so everyone into the classroom!"

He makes a sweeping gesture with his arms as we file ungraciously into the makeshift classroom consisting of too many tables crammed into Therapy Room 1. We have school every weekday.

Elle stands by the window and remarks on the weather, waving a copy of *The Great Gatsby*. I haven't known her long, but she's charged into my life so loudly that it feels like she's been a permanent fixture the whole time. Like a rechargeable battery. When I'm around her, problems are eclipsed by a haze of positivity and beauty. Elle makes time go faster because she has so much to say and to think about that there aren't enough minutes in every day, so she ignores the constraints of night and day, because there are more important things to do, to be, to hope for.

She is everyone's lifeboat, an amber whirlwind of life, the only one who can navigate the realities of madness. The only one who can get us singing ABBA into the dodgy karaoke microphone, rousing people with impassioned speeches like we are an army fighting a war. I suppose in some ways we are; it's just a different kind of war. Maybe that's why I don't tell anyone that she isn't taking her medication, because maybe then she'll stay how she is, colorful and dancing in the corridors at midnight, even though I know that things are only going to go one way.

"You can actually see the wind rustling through the trees," she says now. "I can see the wind."

"How? There aren't any leaves," I say.

"You don't need leaves to see the wind," she replies quaintly, the pages of *The Great Gatsby* opening in a fan.

"That's lovely, Elle," says Maureen, the half-sighted English teacher with grizzled hair and a limp. "Let's have a seat and you can think about wind imagery, then. Jasper, do you have your essay on Mr. Dorian Gray?"

Jasper passes over a dog-eared piece of A4 paper. "Elle ate the rest of it, sorry," he says with a smirk in Elle's direction.

"Oh, dear," wheezes Maureen earnestly, "you really shouldn't do that, Elle, paper will give you terrible indigestion . . ."

"So sorry," says Elle. "It won't happen again. It's just, you know, I get so hungry sometimes that I can't contain myself. I just eat the first things I see: Jasper's homework, pen lids, knitting wool . . ."

"She ate a furball once," I add.

"Oh, yeah," breathes Elle, as if a fond memory has dawned upon her. "I ate the therapy cat's furball. Tasted like mustard."

"A furball?" splutters Maureen, horrified. "No, you mustn't eat furballs, Elle."

"I'll try," says Elle, very seriously. Jasper snorts.

"Stop," I whisper to Jasper, stifling an explosion of laughter. "You're scaring her."

On the other side of Therapy Room 1, Alice is deep in a conversation with John, the substitute teacher, about the reproductive system of chimpanzees. She is spending days at a time at home in the middle of the week, has been promoted to the Sapphire table, and is eating everything on her plate, heckling Dr. Flores for a discharge date.

"So what you need to do is draw an annotated diagram . . ." John says.

Obligingly, Alice takes a pencil and pencil sharpener from the tray and begins to draw. Patient Will stands up and leaves, muttering woes to himself. No one stops him.

For the next hour, I stare at a pile of history dates dotted between clumps of text in Comic Sans, but it doesn't sink in. Luckily, the perks of being a mental patient mean that I'm allowed to blame my "difficulty in concentrating" for the fact that I've only written the learning objective itself when Maureen hobbles over to see how much I've done. Elle continues to stand up, barking occasional remarks about Jay Gatsby and Daisy Buchanan and green lights and traffic lights and road accidents to whomever will listen.

"I think it's creepy. I mean, he's essentially just stalking her," she says, standing on one leg. "I wouldn't want to be Daisy."

"Can you please write down your thoughts?" says Maureen testily. "I'd like to see them on paper."

"If she doesn't eat it first," says Jasper under his breath, and Maureen shoots him a look.

When the clock finally hits three thirty, Elle is the first to dart out of the room and into the dining room for a snack. Jasper follows with a grim expression. Soft cheese and bread sticks. It takes him forty-five minutes to finish it.

There's a new ice-cream parlor, just ten minutes away from Lime Grove. "How lucky is that?" says Nurse Will. "Not all recovering anorexics get to go to an ice-cream parlor, you know."

He's taken me, Jasper, and Elle.

The parlor is called Mrs. Moonshine's. The surfaces are still wooden and unpainted and covered in screwdrivers, and there is one saw propped up in the corner. The blackboard behind the counter drips promises of caramel and spiced fruits and peppermint ice cream smothered in melted chocolate.

"You all right?" I ask Jasper, who is holding his hands clenched tight by his sides to conceal his shaking.

"Yeah," he says with a forced grin. "It looks good." But I know he can only see the calories leeching out of the chalk and seeping into his skin.

"You can just ask for it without the caramel," I say. "Elle can do it for you. She's doing it for me."

"We're as pathetic as each other." He laughs gratefully. If he isn't the one who orders the scoop of syrupy vanilla ice cream, then he isn't supposed to feel guilty. He doesn't ask for it, or choose which sickly calorific flavor out of twenty to have. He has a thought process. I'm just awkward.

Elle pays ten pounds all in shining silver coins because Nurse Will wants to get rid of his change. The woman behind the counter grumpily counts every last five pence with stumpy fingers before slipping them into her Italian-flag apron with a grunt.

Elle and I share a tower of ginger ice cream and real cream-and-ginger-nut biscuits crushed like breadcrumbs over the top, and Jasper obligingly eats his scoop of vanilla ice cream with a teaspoon Nurse Will has brought from the unit in the pocket on his chest. That's Jasper's rule: If he misses breakfast, he will eat every single other meal with no complaints or rolling of eyeballs.

"I think we should go do something," says Jasper as he clangs down his teaspoon with a flourish. He hasn't scraped out the pool of ice cream that has melted at the bottom of the bowl.

"I don't think so," says Nurse Will. "You're on sit-down."

"Seriously?" Now Jasper does roll his eyes (the meal is settling in his stomach and he's allowed to complain). "I just ate ice cream. That means I should be able to forfeit a sit-down."

"It's great that you ate it, but don't wind me up. A sit-down is a sit-down."

They're both winding each other up. Jasper is going to do his sit-down, but Nurse Will isn't going to make him.

"Fifteen minutes? Then a lap of the park before going back to the unit?"

Nurse Will tuts and shakes Jasper's hand. "You drive a hard bargain, young man."

I think every psychiatric ward needs a Nurse Will.

Nurse Will times exactly fifteen minutes on the stopwatch on his phone and as it beeps we stand up with scraping chairs and swiftly leave the shop, the woman behind the counter waving with her stumpy fingers as we go.

"One lap only at a leisurely pace, am I understood?"

"You're so unprofessional," says Elle airily as she slips her hands into gloves. They're decorated with reindeers that have bobble noses.

"She's joking," says Jasper.

It is true, though—Nurse Will *is* unprofessional. He shouldn't take us on a walk around the park, past the creaking swings still wet from last night's frost and the disused skate park decorated in patternless graffiti, but we aren't going to complain. A lap around the park is like gold for the strange people who are locked away night and day.

So we don't tell anyone about our walk among the frozen cigarette ends and dying tangles of ivy, among the shards of sunlight, because Nurse Will could get kicked out of the unit quicker than it takes us to finish our lap, and we'd be stuck with no one but ever-changing figures in nursing uniforms swapping shifts at every chime of the clock.

But he's given us a taste for freedom.

Overnight it snows. The nurses open the door to the garden in the morning, and the sharp air spills in as they let us out.

We play in the snow like eight-year-olds. We are teenagers, all of us, but, locked away in the madhouse, who can judge us for making snowmen all morning long? We aim snowballs at the half-open window of Dr. Flores's office, and it isn't until Jasper gets one in and it splatters against the grubby carpet that he sticks his head out with a weird expression on his face. I think he's smiling. Perhaps he is puzzled that it seems the snow has managed to cure us of our sadness in one day, and our flushed faces snorting at him are enough for him to spend the rest of the day pondering. He waves as he shuts his window and returns to his desk.

The Great Escape is Elle's idea, but it takes the three of us to manufacture it. We sit at the bottom of the garden when everyone else has gone in, next to the withered potted plants, a relic of the failed Gardening Club.

"This fence isn't even high. If we wanted to run away, they couldn't stop us," says Elle.

At first, I'm not sure if she's joking. Sometimes she's hard to read. Iris painted on the flicks in her eyeliner so nobody could tell what was going on underneath. She was silent, and Elle wears her heart on her sleeve, but they're both as mysterious as each other.

"It's just roads behind it—I can see from my room. Ten seconds and we'd be gone."

"I'd give it twenty," says Jasper, a grin forming. "Twenty seconds to freedom." His black hair tumbles over his eyes and he brushes it back impatiently.

"Look," Elle continues, standing up, "we just move this bench closer to the fence and we're halfway there. We should do it."

I said the snow brings out a different side to people, didn't I?

"Let's do it," I say, holding out my hand for the other two to shake simultaneously.

"Now?" says Jasper, jumping up and grinning.

Elle raises her eyes and looks at me. I shrug.

"Where are we going to go?" I ask.

"Don't have a fucking clue," Elle replies, walking over to the bench with her hand in mine. "Who cares, anyway?"

Elle's right. She doesn't have a fucking clue at all.

The fence is harder to get over than we anticipate. The snow has softened the wood so it's slippery and difficult to get a grip, and as I grasp the top of it I can feel a metal nail digging into the palm of my left hand. My legs flail, scraping against the wood, trying to find a hold.

"Hang on," says Jasper, "I'll give you a leg up."

"I'll do it," says Elle, cupping my boot in her hands. "You're 'physically compromised,' Jasper, don't forget."

"Shut up," Jasper snaps, but he's laughing. "Just hurry up."

I swing my legs over until I'm hanging on the other side from my arms, my rib cage pressed hard against the fence. Once I let go, the ground is farther than I think and I land in the snow, winded.

I groan and hear laughter from the other side of the fence.

"Come on, then, otherwise I'm going to be the only one in trouble," I say.

"Actually, we've changed our minds—see you later, Tay," I hear Elle say from the other side of the fence, but before I have time to react Jasper clambers over and joins me.

"Only joking," he says.

I stick out my tongue. Elle follows with a light nimbleness, landing softly in the snow.

"Welcome to the world beyond," she says, opening her arms and presenting to us the grimy parking lot.

"Not exactly the promised land," Jasper says. "We better run."

It's difficult to sprint when your lungs are choking on laughter, and I'm left spluttering for breath before we even leave the drive. There is something elating about the day— the icy sunlight, the frozen trees, the cool breath of each inhalation of freedom—that makes me want to spin and scream with giddy excitement, our frozen footsteps in the snow.

And as we turn and run out of the hospital gates, I'm

pretty sure I hear the emergency alarm start to screech. That's another thing—I'm not sure why the gates are open.

The main road is almost deserted because of the snow, and we run through the middle of it along the grit, our shoes crunching on the ground, with each step my heart thumping faster with exhilaration and stress.

"I can't believe we've done this!" Jasper says, above heavy breaths.

Elle laughs and spins in circles, her hands extended to the sky. The trees lining the road are heavy with snow, their gnarled brown branches hanging limply under the weight.

"We're fucking free!" she shouts, and grabs my hand as we run through the empty street, our feet soaking from the carpet of sludge.

We finally come to a stop in an alley twenty minutes later. Panting, Jasper crouches down on the pavement, his skinny hands pale and bare in the gray light.

"Where are we?" he says, looking up at Elle.

"Not a clue," she says. "Doesn't really matter, though, does it? We can do whatever the hell we want."

"How long before you reckon they'll start looking for us?"

"I bet they already are," I say, remembering the alarm. "The police will probably find us soon."

"Don't be so defeatist," says Elle, and we start walking again, following the alley as it thins out and meets the road again. Jasper and I follow Elle as she turns onto a cycle path heading away from the road.

It takes us an hour to reach the countryside, walking slowly and deliberately until we see a thick clump of woodland squatting over the track.

"It's so beautiful," chatters Elle. "The world is so beautiful, and we are invincible!" She takes my hand again, giggling, her eyes alight with the kind of frenzied happiness that comes from too much snow and too little medication.

It begins to snow again, lightly, flakes falling in the milky light. You can hear the hum of the distant motorway like a nest of bumblebees, but there is nothing near here. A magpie squawks and lands on the path in front of us. One for sorrow. I vaguely look for another one, see a pigeon and decide that will do. I don't think about the police catching us. I don't think about my problems, or Dr. Flores, or Iris. There is nothing to think about. There are no worries. There is only freedom.

I turn to Elle and Jasper. Jasper's skinny body is shivering. His lips are gray.

"I'm really fucking cold," he says.

Elle finds it funny. She peels off her jumper and passes it to him as he breathes in small pockets of air between shudders.

"We've hardly been out for long, Jasp, don't die on us!"

Jasper stabs his middle finger up through the folds in the fabric of her jumper. "Whose stupid idea was this again?" he says.

"Elle's," I say. "If you die, blame her, not me."

"You were my accomplice! I haven't killed Jasper all on my own, I don't take all the credit," Elle replies as she continues to skip ahead, unsettling the snow and tossing it up in a cascade of powdery flakes as she goes. "Look, you can't complain, anyway—we can see the whole world!"

The motorway sprawls ahead of us, a seething scar of gray slashed across the landscape. The faint drone of exhausts and engines shudders across the snow.

"It's a road," says Jasper. "It's a road and it's ugly and we need to turn around."

"Don't be silly, we can't turn around. Come on!" says Elle, her face flashing with a reckless energy, her fingers still tightly entwined in mine like a small child. Sun glints off the snow in a hazy reflection. The clouds are etched into smiles. The world is smiling. Elle is smiling. Even Jasper is smiling, because we're free. If this is what it feels like to be on the run, I can manage that. If being on the run is surges of exhilaration and spontaneity and screams of delight, then I can manage that.

The snow ends as we meet the motorway. Wisps of exhaust fumes and screeching and Jasper clutching my shoulder. Horns bellow, two of them, three, four. Jasper shouts something into my ear but I keep running, my arms stretched upward into the air, surrendering to the hood of each car, but nothing hits. Sprinting, sprinting, gasping breaths of cold petrol air, eyes fixed on the middle of the motorway, Jasper's fingers digging in. I search desperately for Elle, for a flash of her ginger hair. There is no Elle.

I lurch for the thin strip of pavement in the middle of the motorway, scramble into it.

"Elle!"

A driver in a pristine Jaguar rolls down his window and swears. Cars pick up speed again. Jasper lets go of my top, panting like a dog.

"Where is she?" he says.

I groan. My heart is punching its way out of my chest.

"I knew . . . I knew this would happen." I knew someone was going to get hurt. Jasper nods as if he knows what I am talking about. We stand, facing the first half of the motorway that we've just crossed.

"Knew what would happen?"

"Elle!" My voice cracks. I pull her into an awkward hug, her forehead knocking against my jawbones.

"It's that anxiety of yours," she says with a grin. "Always catastrophizing. I've been here longer than you two."

I laugh but it sounds weak. "I thought you were dead."

"I know," she says airily. "I saw."

"Don't be an idiot," I say.

She takes my hand in hers like she always does. "Sorry." She doesn't mean it.

"We need to get to the other side," says Jasper eventually.

"Yeah."

For the next stretch of road, I am the one clutching the fabric of Elle's top as she nimbly snakes her way through angry cars. We make it across to the other side in twenty seconds, twenty long and stressful seconds broken only by more slamming brakes and screaming horns.

"Shit," says Jasper as we start to clamber up the other side of the bank, under the gnarled branches of snow-laden trees. "Whose stupid idea was that?"

We walk through a fleecy white field, toward a distant cluster of houses that signals civilization. My feet are pierced with needles made from ice. Jasper's teeth chatter.

"Let's find a road," says Elle brightly, apparently unaffected.

"Seriously?" snaps Jasper. "We just got *off* a road. We could have died."

"We weren't going to die," says Elle dismissively. "Anyway, I don't mean that sort of road. You're cold, and I have an idea."

Don't get into vans with strange men, kids. That's what I'm thinking when Elle prances into the middle of the road, thumb raised in the air, and the first car to stop is a battered Volkswagen camper van, driven by a bearded middle-aged man with a bandanna, two eyebrow piercings, and an oversized leather jacket.

"Oh, for Christ's sake," mutters Jasper as Elle leans into his open window, grinning like a Cheshire cat on ecstasy. Across the hood of the camper van is a scarlet cartoon image of Ziggy Stardust.

"He'll take us!" Elle shouts delightedly. "Let's go!"

"We can't just get into a car with a random man," I hiss.

"Oh, stop being so boring. He's nice, he's going to drop us in town!" Her flushed face looks earnest.

"He's wearing a bandanna," says Jasper quietly.

"So? What's that got to do with anything?" she says sharply. I roll my eyes.

"Oi, are you lot coming?" calls the man, leaning out of the van.

"We can't stay here, Jasper looks like he's at death's door, let's just go. It'll be fun!" With that she links arms with Jasper and manhandles him toward the van. He turns to me with a bewildered expression.

"I can't believe you," I say as Elle slides open the door with a flourish. But I follow her.

The camper van is small and cramped inside. A grill coated with the blackened remains of a barbecue lies on one of the seats, and piles of unwashed clothes are dumped in one corner.

"Just move everything out the way," says the man as he turns the radio down. Some Queen song.

Elle slams the door on Jasper and me and dives into the front seat. "I'm Elle," she says brightly. "And that's Jasper, and Tamar."

"Ralph," he grunts.

Jasper continues to shiver under Elle's thin jumper. As Ralph revs the engine and begins to trundle over the grit, the nauseating smell of burning rubber wafts into my nostrils. An empty cage that once must have housed some small animal clanks on the floor as we move.

"Wine gum?" He passes a packet behind him.

Don't get into vans with strange men, kids—especially not if they offer you sweets. Hmm. Let's hope they're not drugged.

The snow-covered hills in the distance merge into one huge expanse of white as Ralph presses down on the accelerator and we trundle back toward the town. He turns the radio up when Elle starts a political debate.

"We need nuclear weapons, though—there are some crazy people out there . . ."

"Sweetheart, you obviously don't know a lot about the world, so why don't you keep your opinions to yourself?"

Elle told me that Dr. Flores had said she was having delusions, delusions that meant she was special and invincible. "What bullshit," I'd said, because Elle is the most special and invincible person that I know. She'd laughed. "He doesn't know a thing, does he?" she'd said.

Two thoughts come into my head now. Either I have been seeing Elle as more wonderful and invincible than she really is, or she is seeing herself as such. Either way, someone is deluded. Not for the first time today, I curse myself for not telling anyone that she's been spitting out her medication.

We swerve across a roundabout and into town.

"Where do you want to get out?" Ralph says, turning to Jasper and ignoring Elle as she continues to babble about the pros and cons of recycling.

"Here's fine," says Jasper hastily. "Thanks a lot." He

unclips his seat belt and jumps out of the van as quickly as he can.

"Your friend's a weird one, isn't she?" Ralph whispers to me as I make to leave.

"Oh, yeah, don't mind her," I say with a smile as I jump out after Elle. "She's just clinically insane. Thanks for the lift!"

"You do realize they'll kill us if we go back?" Elle says, running a finger across her throat.

"Come on, we have to," I say. "You, especially, have to— you're sectioned. No offense . . ."

Elle gives me a look, but she isn't angry. "Don't be so boring. They can't force me to go back."

I sigh, because that's exactly what they can do. That's where Jasper and I have the upper hand. We are voluntary patients (which means if you do as you're told and stay here even though you don't want to, we won't section you). Elle, on the other hand, is tied to Lime Grove with the hefty shackles of the law.

Everyone else will be having afternoon snack by now: two yogurts and an apple (chopped up, of course) for Alice, if she manages to avoid a packet of crisps, like she usually does. Leftover crisps collect over weeks for everyone else. Then they'll be going into art group together, and they'll sit in a circle around the art table and Alice will probably paint Patient Will's hand with acrylic paint, as if it's henna. It might be unbearably tedious, but at least I could ask Emma for a cup of tea with milk and two sugars, and at least it would be warm.

The police car is on the pavement in front of us before we have time to react. Its blue lights are still flashing as two police officers barge out of the car and round us up.

The first police officer is so burly, he looks as if he is going to burst out of his bullet-proof vest at any second.

"What the hell do you think you're playing at?" he shouts. "We've had half the fucking police force out looking for three missing teenagers. And a shitting air ambulance." It's fair to say he is not pleased. "Fucking hell."

"So," says the second police officer. "What've you got to say for yourselves? I warn you, it better be good."

At this, Elle chooses, as she always does, a spectacularly inappropriate time to burst into a fit of helpless laughter.

"It really isn't funny. Haven't you got phones?"

"No, we don't," says Jasper as I try to give Elle a cold but subtle glare while the policemen aren't watching. I think it makes her worse.

The second policeman snorts. "No phones? How old are you? Sixteen? Don't give me that bullshit, one of you must have a phone."

"Get in the car," says the burly one.

We sit, squashed awkwardly into the back seat, and the policemen climb into the front, bellowing into their walkie-talkies.

"Yeah, we've got them. No worries. Over."

"Nice day, was it?" says the second policeman. "Running across motorways?"

"We're really sorry," says Jasper quietly.

I nod in agreement and try to ignore Elle as she struggles to keep a straight face. The police car smells of petrol and glacé cherries, possibly from the cheap-looking air freshener hanging on the front mirror. The first policeman sighs pointedly.

"I don't doubt that. Probably not seeming like such a funny idea now, eh?"

"No."

"Right, let's get you idiots back home, then," says the second policeman, pulling the car into gear and swerving into the middle of the road.

"Who lives closest?"

"We, um, we live together," I cut in.

"You lot related?" he says skeptically, turning around and eyeing us.

"Oh, no, we just—" begins Jasper.

"We're from the psychiatric hospital . . . Lime Grove," says Elle. She seems to have composed herself.

Like that, the demeanor of the two policemen changes. The first policeman nods, then turns back around and gives us a crooked smile. He has a gold tooth on the right side of his mouth.

"Well, I hope you had a good day on the outside, you three, but we're going back to lockdown," he says as the car jerks and we head down the slushy road, back to Lime Grove.

The reception we receive when we arrive back at Lime Grove is icier than the weather we've just been out in. Dr. Flores has gone home, but an army of angry nurses in blue are waiting for us, rage on their faces. The policemen look more scared than we are of Emma's pulsing temples and widened eyes, and they leave us as soon as we've been let in, muttering that their work here is done and they need to go. Emma doesn't need to say a word to make herself painfully clear. I wish that Elle would stop smirking and fidgeting as we sit on the chairs in the reception, waiting to be searched, one by one.

"Tamar," says Emma icily, ushering me through the first air-lock door without making eye contact. "Take off your shoes. And your jumper and bra."

I do as I am told. Emma doesn't say anything more, but she has a grim expression on her face as she swipes me down with the metal detector, feels the soles of my shoes. The silence is loud.

"Sorry . . ." I venture as Emma feels the padding of my bra.

"You've been incredibly immature," snaps Emma. "I don't want to hear any more from you three for the rest of the evening."

So that's that. We are sent to our rooms without dinner (apart from Jasper, he has to have dinner, of course), like naughty children. Elle giggles all the way into her bed.

THEN

The first time I slept on the floor of my bedroom in my clothes, I woke to the faint burning smell of a cigarette I had stubbed out on my carpet. Brew, the dog, had found his way next to me and was sitting upright, panting and wheezing next to my ear. I reached a hand out and squeezed his collar. The dress I'd been wearing was crumpled. I got to the open window and pulled it shut; a sharp breeze had begun to blow into the room with the dawn. My head throbbed, and I put it down to the cigarettes. I could feel their smoky presence still sitting in my throat. Slowly and methodically, I peeled off the dress, its corners encrusted with dry sweat, threw it into the growing pile of unwashed clothes on my chair. Anxiety means you go through clothes quickly. I crawled into bed.

The monster had started with a pair of nail scissors, a small scratch, and an ouch. But now it had grown.

Later, when it was lighter, my bedroom door swung open, hitting the chest of drawers. My dad was dressed in the pink shirt that Mum hated and he leaned on the door with a revolted expression on his face.

"It smells like a bloody tobacco factory in here, Tamar," he said, walking over to the window and reopening it. "We told you not to smoke indoors. It's not difficult, really, is it?"

"It was out of my window . . ." I said lamely, sitting up and digging my fingers into Brew's fur.

"Don't give me that. If you have to smoke, you've got to do it in the garden, end of."

"Sorry. I'm sorry," I said.

He sighed. "You've got school in half an hour, anyway, so you better get ready."

"OK, I'll get ready," I said.

Uniform on: crumpled shirt, stiff tie, blazer with too-short arms.

I said I wouldn't leave the house by myself ever again, but sometimes it isn't good to give yourself the choice, especially when you're prone to making the wrong ones.

Dad gave me a lift because I'd stopped taking public transport on my own. Fear had become my natural state of being.

"Thanks," I said as I got out of the car.

The walk from the school gates to the front reception was exactly one hundred yards. I counted my steps.

I sat at the back of a history classroom rolling cigarettes, a small pyramid building behind my pencil case. Rolling cigarettes and talking. Vaguely aware of my mouth opening and shutting. The topic of the day: sandwiches vs. wraps.

Now, if you think about it, a wrap is far more diverse—you can put all the same stuff in a wrap as a sandwich, the difference being (besides their superior taste) that when toasted, you have to call a sandwich a panini or toastie or something, whereas a wrap still remains the same, unadulterated thing that it was to begin with. Although it's fair to say that you can't have a jam wrap—that's weird. So perhaps sandwiches still have the upper hand . . .

It was starting to become more of a monologue. I did this a lot, I think. I wasn't zoned out, quite the opposite. It didn't take long before the familiar panic began to build in the base of my stomach. I scanned the room: heads down and furious scribbling, ignoring me.

All I had to do was copy the words in front of me. Take notes: *In World War II, conscription was implemented . . .*

I can't do it.

Why don't I understand?

Maybe I should get up and leave.

Or burst into tears.

Or both.

No, no, no.

I'm the only person in this classroom who can't do it.

The rest of the class are going to pass their history A-level and I'm not. I'm not.

I used to be good at history. What went wrong?

"I can't do this; it's actually impossible."

"Yes, you can, Tamar." A note of exasperation in Mr. Peters's voice. "And get rid of those cigarettes, please, or I'll do it for you."

When I'm anxious, I can talk for England; when I'm really anxious, I am silent and paralyzed and small.

Toby scribbled furiously, his elbow jutting out. He knew what he was doing.

Mia hunched low over her book, her hands moving swiftly across the page. She knew what she was doing.

Everyone knows what they are doing.

I'm the only one in the whole classroom, the whole

world, who is lost and frightened and confused and can't understand the PowerPoint on conscription.

Cardiac arrest, myocardial infarction, heart attack. I felt it coming in the minutes before it happened—a sudden sputtering and shuddering of the pulse in my chest. My hands tingled, and I felt the blood as it stopped, pressing up against a blockage, swelling under the pressure. I knew I was going to die.

The scream came out shrill and weak but it still pierced the rustling-paper quiet of the classroom as I collapsed with a crash on the floor, my chair flipping up and clanging down as I fell. My chest was on fire: a sharp, raw pain coursing through the gaps in my rib cage and up toward my collarbone, a torrent of lava gushing through my veins and into my aorta and into my heart.

"What the fuck, Tamar?" said Mia, jumping to her feet.

"Call an ambulance," I yelled hoarsely. "My heart is stopping!"

"Oh my God, no it's not. Stop with the theatrics," Mia said.

"Can you sit up?" said Mr. Peters, kneeling beside me. "Toby, go and fetch the nurse."

"No!" I cried. "I'm dying."

"Just take a deep breath . . . Breathe in. And breathe out. In. Out . . ."

How many fifteen-year-old girls have heart attacks? In. Out. How many of them then die on the floor of a classroom?

The school nurse hurtled in, a first-aid kit in hand. She looked like someone who'd been waiting for this moment her whole life.

"If you'll just pop your sleeves up for me," she said, brandishing a blood-pressure cuff.

"What?"

Toby and Mia and Mr. Peters and every other bloody pupil in the room stared at me.

"Come along, I need to check your blood pressure," the nurse repeated impatiently, tapping her knee. "Roll them up."

"No," I snapped, backing away from the cuff. "I'm

feeling better. I'm fine." I didn't feel fine. My ears were ringing.

"You weren't fine a second ago," said Mia.

"That's enough, Mia," Mr. Peters said warningly.

"Come along, roll them up, please. I need to check your blood pressure. You said you were dying."

The next decision shattered the fragile mask I'd been wearing—you can only wear masks for so long—and destroyed everything that was normal and safe and close to me.

She pulled my school jumper over my elbows and up to my shoulders. Strands of fluff from the lining stuck to the hairs on my arms as the sleeves bunched up.

A silent gasp tiptoed through the room.

"What the fuck have you done to your arm?" said Mia.

The school nurse didn't take my blood pressure.

"I think you had better come with me," she said.

Mia didn't like me when we first met, age six. She pushed over the Jenga tower that I had built in the quiet area of the playground, with its tiled walls and patterned tarmac, then ran over to the nearest teacher, tears fluttering among her camel eyelashes, and accused me of pushing over her Jenga tower, the one she'd worked ever so hard on. When the teacher came over to reprimand me, I picked up the nearest block of wood and hurled it toward Mia's head. It didn't reach her head, though. It just landed a few inches away from her shoes.

"Tamar!" The teacher had frog-marched me to the "naughty wall," the wall where I would pay for my heinous crime, and stood me up against it for the rest of break time. My fingers traced the rough dips of cement surrounding the iron-red bricks. I still remember how it felt against my six-year-old fingernails, and the tears that soaked into my crinkled school dress as I watched Mia tackle the boys in a game of football like I'd always been too scared to do. She stuck out her tongue at me when she saw me looking, grinning like a china doll come alive. It wasn't only that Mia didn't like me at first. I didn't like her, either.

We were forced into a friendship by Toby, really, when he knelt on one knee, the knee that was grazed and dusted in crumbled dirt and remnants of mud, and proposed to her in that same quiet area. She fluttered her eyes in the same way, in a way that a six-year-old shouldn't know how to do. Toby told her that she was the prettiest girl in the school, and that he was in love with her.

"You have to be friends with Tamar, too, though," he had said as he squirmed away from a kiss she planted on his forehead. "If we're getting married, Tamar has to be your friend, too."

"OK," Mia said. She'd taken my hand in hers and clasped it tightly, too tightly, and smiled at me. "We can be friends." Her nails dug into my palms.

NOW

"OK, I've got the vinegar," says Elle as Jasper loiters suspiciously outside Therapy Room 1.

"What're you doing?" he asks. You can almost see his ears prick up in interest.

"We're playing a game," says Elle brightly. "Want to join?"

Jasper sidles in and closes the door.

"Why do you have sachets of vinegar?"

"It's obvious, isn't it?" Elle says with an exaggerated eye roll.

"Is it?" Jasper rolls his eyes back at her.

"Well, we're using vinegar instead of vodka. We each have to say three things about ourselves and someone else has to guess which one is a lie."

"And the vinegar comes in where . . . ?"

"It's a forfeit," she says impatiently, aggressively tossing her hair behind her ears. "Sit down." She grabs his ankles and he collapses into the beanbag chair beside her.

"All right, all right . . ."

"I'll go first!" Elle says, tossing a greasy packet of vinegar over to me. "OK . . . I'm half-Irish, I like spaniels, and my mum was a whore."

"Er . . ." I turn awkwardly to Jasper, who shrugs with his eyebrows.

"It's easy." She giggles.

"I don't know—you don't like spaniels?"

"No! I'm half-Welsh, not Irish."

"How is that easy?" mutters Jasper grumpily as I peel open the vinegar and pour it into my mouth, forcing back my gag reflex as it gouges into the wounds in my mouth where I've bitten the insides of my cheeks in my sleep.

"Shut up," I say when they laugh at my grimacing.

"Your go, Jasper," natters Elle, juggling with the packets in front of her.

"Erm, well." He rubs his chin. "I have a beer-bottle-lid collection in my bedroom at home—"

"A beer-bottle-lid collection?" Elle snorts. "Why?"

"Don't interrupt," says Jasper snarkily. "I haven't finished. I have a pet snake and I love food."

"Well, it's obviously the last one." I laugh. "I mean, no offense . . ."

"Get yourself another pack of vinegar, then, Tay," Jasper says smugly. "Nobody said I don't love food."

"Yeah, he just doesn't eat it," says Elle knowingly.

"It's so disgusting, though," I grumble as I hold my nose and squirt the vinegar onto my tongue.

"Go, it's your turn," says Elle, with a swift clap of her

hands. Things always go too slowly for Elle. She is the chee-tah in a world full of overfed house cats.

"Oh . . ." Who am I? What is there to say about me? Tamar? Sometimes I'm not even sure whether that name has anything to do with me. What makes me? "I run. I can run, sometimes. Once my friend locked me in the garden shed for three hours when I was younger, and I've killed someone with my bare hands." I say three truths. What is wrong with me?

"Shit. Deep," says Elle.

Jasper points a finger at me. "I knew it," he says. "I said you were a psychopath as soon as I met you!"

I give a hollow laugh. "You called it."

"The lie is that you can run!" says Elle with a grin.

"No," I say. "I'm actually a convicted murderer."

"Don't worry, we still love you just as you are," Jasper says.

Would they, though? If they really believed it, would they?

Nurse Will swings into the room without knocking. "Just doing checks. Everything good in here?"

"No, Tamar's a murderer," says Elle.

"Oh, she is, is she?" Nurse Will gives a bark of sardonic laughter. "Try not to finish these two off as well, then, will you? Oh, Elle, Dr. Flores wants to see you in his office."

Elle jumps up with a groan.

I'll try. I really will. But I've killed a friend before, so I can't make any promises.

He's out of the room with the clipboard at his side before I have time to respond.

Jasper and I sit in silence for a few minutes before he slips the vinegar packets into his pocket.

"Green tea?" he says.

We sneak into the nurses' kitchen—one of the agency nurses forgot to lock the door. Jasper stands on the lookout. It's possible to see directly into the nurses' office from the window in the door; they are sitting in a circle talking about something. Probably the weather. They like to talk about the weather. *Nice day today, isn't it? Bit chilly, though.* Of course, the weather doesn't matter to us, because we barely go out.

"For fuck's sake, hurry up, Tamar," Jasper says, turning around. I laugh.

"It's not my fault—the kettle's taking ages! Just move away from the window so they don't see you."

The kettle steams and rumbles and clicks. I pour the boiling water into polystyrene cups and laugh again. It is stupid. I'm laughing because I am boiling water to make tea.

"Let's go." Jasper dramatically sweeps open the door and ushers me past as if we're part of an important secret operation.

"Stop being an idiot and get the door," I snap, and he sticks his tongue out at me.

"All right, Mum."

We've held the door to the bedroom corridors open with a rolled-up newspaper, and no one has noticed, because chats about the weather in the nurses' office are far more important. We go into Jasper's room, stick a Maroon 5 poster over the viewing slat with Blu Tack, and lock the door, which is pretty pointless because it can be opened from the outside anyway. But somehow it makes it more exciting. Jasper takes two crinkled teabags out of his suitcase.

"How did you get them in?" I ask.

"Hid them down below," he says, pulling up his T-shirt and snapping the elastic on his boxers.

"Are you joking? I'm not using them!" I say, throwing him a look of disgust, before seeing him grin. "You're disgusting."

We sit on the floor next to the wardrobe and brew the tea for longer than necessary, until it is no longer green but a sludgy brown color.

"Cheers." Jasper winks at me and we both dissolve in helpless laughter at the ridiculousness of the situation.

"We're going to be in so much trouble."

Jasper puts a finger to his lips. "They'll never find us," he whispers.

Of course they do find us. They slam on Jasper's door and call for a response but we are too involved in our green-tea-drinking high to care. Instead Jasper just climbs into the wardrobe and shuts the door, so that when one of the nurses sets off the emergency alarm and four of them burst into the room at the same time, it is me they round upon.

"What are you doing in here? This isn't your room. Where's Jasper?"

Two more nurses dash in.

"Sorry, I'll go."

"Hang on a minute, Tamar, what is going on here?"

I'm still smirking, but they aren't laughing. The alarms still screech through the building, ricocheting off the walls. A few patients peer through the open door.

"Nothing, nothing, we were just—"

"We?" says Emma. "Who is 'we'?" As she speaks, the agency nurse, who'd left the kitchen door unlocked in the first place, opens the wardrobe. Jasper stares guiltily out at the room, his black hair unkempt around his shoulders. He is curled up in a corner, as if that will hide him. I see him blushing, and as I stumble to leave I knock over a cup of tea.

The nurses don't find our antics funny. They leave Jasper to clear up the spilled green tea from his bedroom floor with tissues from the bathroom, and they send me down to talk to Dr. Flores, who does not look up to greet me; he carries on tidying his desk when I walk in. His office is always untidy, and I've never seen him tidying it, so it seems strange that he's chosen now to do it. I guess he just can't be bothered to give me the time of day.

"We—myself and my colleagues—are trying to run a hospital, Tamar. A hospital is somewhere that people come to get better. Had you realized that?" The cold sarcasm in his voice shocks me. "Since you've come here, you seem to be hell-bent on breaking every rule that we've put in place for your safety. Why?" He packs a pile of notes into a folder and moves it aimlessly to the other side of the desk.

"I haven't been breaking rules. I want to go home."

He turns and raises his eyebrows at me. "Jasper, as I'm sure you know, has an eating disorder, and we have certain rules about things like tea, or chewing gum, which I know you've also been giving to people, because some of our patients use these to escalate their self-destructive behaviors. Did that occur to you? Did it occur to you that the rules we have in place here are not solely for your inconvenience?"

I am a naughty schoolchild in a headmaster's office. A convicted criminal before a judge.

"No," I reply lamely. "Sorry."

He doesn't respond. Instead he sits in silence as if he's studying me. Psychiatrists have a good way of doing that: looking at you and somehow managing to make you feel incredibly uncomfortable. Maybe that's a technique designed to get answers out of you. I don't know. It's not very effective.

"What do you want me to do?" he says finally with a sigh. "I'm not going to keep you here if you continue to hamper the progress of other patients."

"Discharge me, then," I snap. "Being here is hampering *my* progress."

"Being here is only what you make of it," he says. "Think about that tonight, will you, and I'll catch up with you next week. Is there anything else you want to ask me?"

I shake my head. "I'm going to bed," I say.

Upstairs, Emma unlocks my bedroom door with a curt "good night" and returns to watching TV in a surly manner, flicking channels from *Supersize vs. Superskinny* to the news. I hear something about terrorist threats muffle through the walls of my room.

I'm the sort of person who things never end well for. I can't even drink a cup of green tea without ruining everyone's day and trying to kill an anorexic patient. I think these thoughts will keep me awake, but they don't. My medication courses through my veins and encases my brain, and I sleep.

"You've got a visitor, Tamar," Nurse Will sings as he saunters into the lounge. "A young man."

"We're not in the eighteenth century," I say.

"Doesn't change the facts," Nurse Will replies, flopping onto his beanbag chair in the corner of the room.

"Is it Toby? I didn't know he was coming."

"Oh, so you know the young man in question?"

"Go away," I snap. "Can you open the door?"

He huffs his way back to standing and unlocks the door with a clank. Toby stands in the hallway, running his fingers through his hair.

"I can leave if this is too . . ."

"No, no. It's a nice surprise."

Something shifts in his face. A muscle underneath his skin or something. Relief, maybe. I smile when he smiles.

"That's good. I just wanted to see how you are, really. I thought about phoning the ward but it didn't feel the same as coming in person . . ."

"We can't stay here," I say, interrupting him before he

enters into a monologue of *War and Peace*. "My room's just up the stairs."

I've never done that before. Had a boy in my room. And I hadn't imagined that the first time would be on a hospital bed with ten centimeters between us and a nurse peering through the viewing slat like we are courting birds in a zoo. But that's just how things turn out.

"So," Toby starts. "How are you? This place seems . . . nice."

"Yeah, we're all categorically crazy, so things can be a little wild at times, but we get by."

He grins as if he isn't sure if he should be grinning. Uncomfortable and jaunty at the same time.

"I'm glad it's not too bad. You know, when Mum told me you were in a . . . mental hospital"—he lowers his voice as if those words are taboo—"I was kind of freaked out. But I'm glad you're getting better."

No one said anything about getting better.

"Look, Tay, there's no point in pretending I don't know about stuff," Toby says, looking directly at me. He's been waiting to say this, I can tell. "Your parents . . . I mean, our parents are pretty close."

I try not to look alarmed. "So, what? You and your parents sit down every evening and gossip about me?"

"Come on, you know it isn't like that. We're just worried about you."

"What do you want me to tell you, then?" I say.

"I just want to know why," he says softly. "I don't understand why."

Of course he doesn't understand why. He's never woken up after a night of scarcely sleeping to another day of barely staying awake with evil, evil, evil hollering in his brain. *What have you done to deserve the right to be alive? Nothing. You're a murderer, and, even worse, you're destroying the lives of everyone around you. You're a burden. Your parents hate you, they'll cry with relief at your funeral, if you even have a funeral, that is. You ungrateful, ugly, selfish, evil piece of shit. Don't get out of bed. Stay under the covers where you're not bothering anyone. Stay under the covers; then, tomorrow, kill yourself.*

"It's hard to explain," I say. "I guess I was just feeling miserable. I hadn't slept well and I had two essays due in. I panicked."

"Oh," he says. "Yeah. We all get miserable. Essays are shit."

I smile at him, because I know he is trying to help. It's not his fault I can't bring myself to talk about it.

"Exactly," I say cheerfully. "It will probably happen to you, too!"

"Great," he says with a laugh. "I look forward to it."

"Did my parents tell you to come?"

"No!" he says indignantly. "I just—I was worried, that's all . . ." He lingers at the foot of my bed.

"It's OK. Sorry. Thanks for coming," I say.

We sit in silence.

"I brought Maltesers," he says suddenly, pulling a crumpled packet out of his jacket pocket. "Can you eat?"

I take one because he looks so miserable and swill it around in my mouth as the chocolate unwraps itself and the biscuit fizzes against my tongue.

"How are you?" I say.

"Good, yeah. Things are good. We won the county championships last week. We thought they would call it off because the hail was chucking it down but it went ahead."

Cross-country is worlds away from Lime Grove. It's everything that Lime Grove isn't: It is messy and open and freeing and fierce and made up of wind and mud and cold air. I used to run with Toby. He is an exercise fanatic, but he could drop everything and get any drug you wanted within an hour and smoke himself into cannabis oblivion the day before a ten-mile race. I don't think I've ever seen him eat a single green vegetable, apart from the time that his mum hid peas in his vanilla ice cream when we were six.

"Where to next, then?" I say. "Nationals?"

"Yeah," he replies. "Gotta go to London."

"That's amazing."

"You should come back some time. You know, when you feel up to it," he says. "We miss you."

He reminds me of the time when I ate one too many Toxic Wastes on the bus journey to a tournament and the driver had to pull over on the hard shoulder so that I could throw them all up on the grass verge, and the whole team had to return home before we arrived at the competition venue. We were twelve then, and Toby was as lanky and gangly as he ever was, boxed into that stage of puberty where he'd stretched up but not out.

He looks different now, as he reminisces about the time when he lost his way on the course and the race had to be called off halfway through. He's filled out with muscle weight and he coughs tar from his chest like he didn't do when he was twelve. His eyes have changed color, too, almost.

It is not until Nurse Will knocks on the door and announces that visiting hours are almost over that I realize I could have studied his face all night—each twitch of his eyelids, rogue hair over his eyes, the defined jawline like strokes on a charcoal drawing.

"Thanks for coming," I say as I walk with him toward the exit. "It was fun."

"Yeah, Tay, there's something I need to mention . . ." he starts. "Mia . . ."

I stop.

"Well, she's been talking about stuff recently, you know, about Iris and the stuff she said, and she wanted to talk about it with you, not for long, you know . . ."

I almost see the lump that Toby swallows in his throat.

We turn toward the waiting room, and there is Elle, bobbing up and down like a rubber duck in a bath, as she always does, and she is talking to someone, a girl with a slight curve at the top of her back, a girl with a brown French braid, twisted over one shoulder. I can see her lips moving, her pencil features hissing syllables into the air. Elle nods and smiles, looks at me, and they laugh together.

Mia's told her something. Elle knows what happened. She knows who I am.

Mia pauses like a cat about to pounce; I know, because I can see her mouth form a static groove in her cheeks.

I go over and sit down, and Elle disappears. Toby hovers

by the door, looking flustered, one leg up like a flamingo, then gives me a quick smile and a wave good-bye.

Mia and I are left, awkwardly sitting on the burgundy chairs, in a silence more unpleasant than a screaming baby.

"Tay—" she starts. "You OK today?"

I've got lockjaw.

"I wanted to come and see you," Mia says. "I know it's a bad day today, and it would probably be playing on your mind."

Time is warped in a psychiatric hospital, but I nod. I know the day. I was just trying not to think about it.

Mia looks at me. "You OK?" she repeats. "Or are you faking it?"

I open my mouth and shut it again. Today is the fourth of March.

On that day years ago, Iris's birthday, it had been Mia's idea to get piercings. She'd had her nipple pierced by the same sleazy guy who'd done my nose ring; no gloves and an electronic cigarette in between his chipped teeth. I'd followed suit because she was right; Mia was always right.

I'm not sure whether she has never liked me, and my madness was the excuse that she'd been looking for to hate me. Whatever it was, she didn't take it well. She took it worse than anyone else.

"You just had to, didn't you?" says Mia suddenly, like she's reading my mind.

"What?"

"You know what," she snaps. "Causing scenes at school, getting yourself here. After Iris."

"Seriously?" I say. "It's not like that . . ."

"I can't actually believe you, Tamar! You just swan around like everything is so much harder for you, when it's not! It's fucking not, OK? Life is shit for everyone, it's shit for me, too, but that doesn't mean we all have to start moping and slitting our wrists for everyone to see. You're a fucking idiot. You just used Iris as an excuse to get attention, everyone can see it. You weren't even close to her. She was just some girl in our class."

"You're not even giving me a chance to—"

"What, so you can revel in yourself and your petty

problems even more?" She stands up, her chair scraping loudly. "No, thanks."

"You can't be serious . . . I didn't choose this . . ."

But she is already at the other side of the waiting room.

"You saw her last, Tamar," she says over her shoulder, slamming the door as she leaves.

I don't have time to focus on my breathing and notice the fast rising and falling of my chest before the world around me begins to crumble into a thousand tiny pixels like a broken TV, and vomit rushes into my brain and I'm heaving like a dying dog on the floor.

"Tay . . ." Elle is crouching down beside me. "It's all right . . ."

"What did she tell you?" I whisper.

I hear Mia being ushered out the front door with a clink of keys and a beep of a code.

Elle laughs. "What are you talking about? I thought she was your friend?"

"Friend? Is that what she said?"

"She said she was your friend, Iris's friend—that it was Iris's birthday. Who's Iris?"

I'm not angry with Toby for bringing her, and I don't know why. Maybe I should be. I'm angry that she's thought to come, that she's thought about the best way to reach me, bringing with her all the memories that I've tried in vain to forget. She blames me for Iris, and so does every other person in the universe. I know it. I'm angry, but she's right.

You killed her. You killed her. You killed her.

THEN

On the fourth of March last year I went into town and bought Iris a birthday present: a bottle of bubble bath. It was impersonal, could have been for anyone. I ate two pints of my feelings in ice cream and watched *Friends*, stared at the blurred shapes on the TV screen, hoping for a cheap laugh to quell the guilt hacking away at my abdomen.

Iris would have been sixteen; legal to smoke and have sex and get married.

I stole that milestone from her. Iris is dead. I am alive.

Later I found myself by the dam. An eerily warm March night, moisture hanging in the air, the snowdrops almost over. Everything was clammy—my socks saturated in warm sweat, my hands sticky with the blood from the dark cuts on my forearm.

The police found me knee-deep in the water, my skirt billowing out in its depths. I didn't put up a fight, so they didn't section me.

Was I going to jump? I don't know.

I spent the night in the ER. They pronounced me sane enough to go home at eight thirty the following morning. The doctors gave me precautionary antibiotics in case the river water that had leached into my cuts gave me septicemia. I didn't take them.

I sat with the school counselor in a room with frosted windows at the back of the school, near the sports hall. It smelled of lavender and crushed orange peel. Brittle cactuses on the desk didn't need watering; they were dead.

Six sessions, once a week, every Thursday, for one hour, during the first half of double French. A "safe place." I said every single thing they wanted to hear from a person turned inward with grief.

I know Iris won't come back, yes. I know she's gone. She's a dead purple-and-yellow flower, crumpled petals curled in on themselves, under the surface of the earth . . .

If I made it poetic and beautiful, the school counselor would not see through the rippling illusion, the lies.

"Will you self-harm again?"

"Of course not. I'm not crazy, honestly."

"Is there something you're not telling me?"

Iris, a flowery ghost girl lying beneath the world with the earthworms, in the soil, blissfully resting in peace. Tamar, a sad and confused friend to the flowery ghost girl . . .

I smoked cigarettes that looked like fireflies as I lit them up and scratched the flaky skin on my arm with the blunt scissors.

Why shouldn't I draw scissors across my skin? Who's to say I don't deserve it?

The school counselor bought my lies, fed them into her eagerly written notes, and after six weeks said I was "OK." The worst was over. I would plummet no further.

Normal life resumed and I went to double French again.

The plummet had already begun.

They all knew. They saw from the way the craters below my eyes were dark tulips against the rough edges of my skin. The anemic blue of the whites of my eyes.

I got moved back a year, came in for one hour a day; one hour on a magenta plastic seat that someone once drew a swastika on incorrectly, so actually it was Hindu and signified something delightful.

One hour of algebra. Solve the quadratic equation $x = $ trips to the sun-frazzled mind + graveyard wanderings. It's easy, Tamar, we did it for GCSE exams, remember? All I had to do was walk the length of the main corridor, try not to be smashed into a locker by the scurry of year sevens hurtling through because they were late for the bell, and enter the math classroom with "Fine" written across my forehead, and talk to no one for fifty-nine minutes. Get up, ignore the homework instructions that my shaken-champagne-bottle head did not have the space for, and go, go, go, leaving the school bell ringing for the next lesson.

No one said a single word to me except for the teacher, who gave me a password on a crumpled scrap of paper for a revision site and told me I'd need it. He didn't tell anyone else that.

And Mia. One minute we were friends, and the next she couldn't bear to look at me. We'd thundered through ten years of a turbulent friendship, but she couldn't handle the monster. I couldn't handle the monster, either.

My mum cried a lot at different times once the monster came. Apparently different tears are actually chemically different; so maybe if you put all the drops of her tears under a microscope you'd find every molecule of every emotion, except happy. She didn't cry happy tears. She was a lot meeker now, too, and she congratulated me even when I didn't deserve congratulations. I went to school for an hour; I hadn't saved the world.

The counselor told me I didn't know myself. She said that I was disconnected and I needed to find my identity, my true personality beneath the drama and the tears and the turmoil. She was wrong. I didn't have identity disturbance; I knew who I was. There are nice people: the ones who help little old ladies cross the road and give sandwiches to homeless people. Then there are the mindless hedonists who love themselves a little too much. Then there are the bad people: the thieves, the serial killers, the mad ax murderers. And then you have me. I was the most dangerous person of all. I knew I was evil.

Every night I checked my wardrobes, under my bed, behind my curtains, just to make sure there was no one lurking, someone planning to avenge Iris by smothering me with pillows in my sleep. I protected myself by sleeping on the floor, curled up like a cat, without any pillows or covers. I put a knife in the drawer of my bedside table. I didn't deserve such obsessive self-preservation, but I did it anyway.

It was strange, I guess, that despite my exhaustive efforts, I couldn't quite protect me from myself.

NOW

I try not to think about Iris after Mia's visit, but when you try not to think about something it usually makes you think about it more. *Iris's birthday is today. Iris is dead. I am alive.*

And . . .

I think of the three razor blades that I smuggled in my hair, but so far have managed to avoid using. I think of other ways out, but hospitals for suicidal people think about things like that carefully. Anti-ligature curtains, anti-ligature doors, baths, sinks, windows that don't open properly. The options for death are limited. I sigh.

And then I know what I am going to do. My fingers skim the battered skin along my left forearm, tracing a long blue line down to my thumb. It protrudes slightly. I walk into the bathroom. I turn the bath tap on, pressing it over and over every twenty seconds as it times out. From my jeans I extract the three razor blades, fresh from the pack.

They didn't search me carefully enough. I hid them on the magnetic curtain rail in my room, in all sorts of other places, too.

I win.

I make three thin scratches on my thigh, watch to see which one draws the most blood. A sort of experiment. I choose the second one, a sharp sense of fear lurching into my stomach. I am scared. I am scared of failing, I am scared of succeeding, I am scared of the mess I will leave behind.

And my palms are sweaty and my heart beats an insane tattoo against my rib cage. Slowly, I begin to undress.

Naked, I walk over to where everyone leaves their body washes. We aren't supposed to leave them around, but we do. I pick out a children's bubble bath. I'm not sure whose it is, but the smell reminds me of childish, carefree, rubber-duck bath times. I squeeze a liberal amount into the bathtub and swirl it around, watching as its amber color dissolves into nothing.

Should I stop?

It's not too late.

Yes, it is. You killed her, you killed her.

I slip into the bath, clutching the small blade. For a few minutes, I lie there, listening to my heavy breathing, smelling the perfume of the bubble bath, thinking about the triangle of thought-feeling-behavior. Trying to piece it together. Of course, now, I think, it doesn't matter.

A nurse knocks on the door. "Just doing checks, Tamar, everything all right in there?"

"Yes, I'm fine, I'm just having a bath, that's all."

I stretch out my arm in front of me and press down, slice the blade across my skin. I watch it split, blood starting to ooze out. I curse. It's not deep enough. I don't stop to think. I should stop to think.

And suddenly I am angry, I am slashing, wildly gashing deeper, deeper into my undeserving body, my self-hatred spewing out as I sprawl in the bath. I am evil. Until, all at once, blood spurts into my face, thick and dark, one spray for every heartbeat, one for every mistake, it clings to my eyelashes, I taste its metallic taste in my mouth and I am screaming, screaming and the blood keeps coming and I know I am going to die, I am going to die and I lurch for the emergency alarm and everything is gone.

My eyes flicker open. The bath is swirling red. A nurse bursts in. I can hear the alarm screeching. Have I pressed it? Have they pressed it?

Am I dead? Am I dead? Seconds falter. Blood spurts.

Someone pulls me up out of the bath. Panicked voices beside me.

Voices from the patients' lounge.

Numb.

A towel is pressed down onto my arm. A undershirt slips over my head.

Dizzy.

I open my eyes. Black spots block my vision. Nausea.

Staggering to the toilet, retching once, twice. Someone holds back my hair.

Red paints the towel, seeping through.

Stumbling blindly to my bedroom, supported by stodgy fingers and someone swearing. Emma, maybe. I'm not sure.

Will it stop? Will the blood stop?

I sit wrapped in a thin towel on my bed and they hold my arm above my head. Blood travels slower when it's traveling up. Tracksuit bottoms pulled up over my legs. I open my eyes.

"That needs stitches."

Blundering to a taxi takes twenty seconds, maybe less.

Feel the shuddering of the engine, a jolt. Lights slowly flash by: reds, ambers, greens.

8:20 p.m.

The dull smell of burning rubber fills my nostrils. Petrol. Mints. Time is slow.

Am I dead? Blood is etched into my mind, oozing through my brain, muffling my senses.

Vomit lingers in my mouth. I swallow. Press down on my arm.

8:30 p.m.

I regain coherence sitting on a hard plastic chair facing an old woman in a purple shirt, who is wearing smudged turquoise eye shadow and a bruised expression.

"You say you did this to yourself?"

I nod. The place where her eyebrows should be is raised. I always get this. The wasting-our-time-and-resources look. She reaches for a pen and writes in swirly, fat writing, "DSH, laceration to left forearm." She draws circles over her *i*'s, not dots. She asks a few more questions: my address, my date of birth, and who is this woman in uniform with you? Oh, you're from the loony bin.

"Is it still bleeding?" I gingerly unwrap the towel. A trail of blood dribbles down and soaks my pants.

"Yeah."

"It's slowed down a lot, though," says Emma.

"In that case, just wait over there, please." She gestures to a cluster of equally uncomfortable-looking chairs on the other side of the room.

Emma takes me over to the corner, next to the vending machines. On the wall next to us is a sign that says TAKE CARE, NOT ANTIBIOTICS and another that says THE ER IS FOR EMERGENCIES. The wall is painted an apricot orange, with cracks where it reaches the shiny floor. Opposite us sits a young man in a soccer uniform with a very swollen wrist and an older man with his wife, who is complaining of chest pains. Outside I see the flashing blue lights of a real emergency.

Suddenly, I begin to feel stupid. The cut is hardly bleeding. I bet they've seen far, far worse. They'll think I'm whining, pathetic.

"Can we just go back to the unit?" I turn to Emma, who is cheerfully taking a piece of strawberry gum out from a packet. "I can dress it there, we've got bandages . . ."

She shoots me an implacable look and I fall silent. I can tell that people are looking at me, looking at the raised, purple scars on my arms, sickened, disgusted. I disgust myself.

We wait for an hour. Emma buys me a bottle of water and a packet of salt and vinegar crisps from the vending machine because she says I look blue. I'm not hungry; the crisps scratch the lining of my throat, but I eat them anyway.

We don't talk.

A baby with a pale face arrives after an hour and twenty-two minutes, her arms cradled tightly around a haggard woman's neck.

After two hours, a nurse comes out of a door at the end of a corridor.

"Tamar?" She is holding a few pieces of paper in her hands.

"At last," mutters Emma, standing up and walking swiftly over to her. I follow.

"Could you just sanitize your hands for me?" the nurse says, pointing at a bottle stuck to the wall.

The nurse is a young woman with dark-brown hair scraped back into a ponytail and three cartilage piercings. She smiles as I awkwardly climb onto the bed, kicking off my shoes. I return the smile weakly. Emma sits down on a folding chair next to the sink. There's a small pot in the corner that has a sticker on it saying CONTAMINATED, SHARP OBJECTS ONLY. I find myself thinking of my blade, submerged in the most definitely contaminated bathwater. There is no way I can salvage it now.

I lose.

I am twisted, OK. I know.

"Tamar, can I have a quick look at your arm?"

I pull off the towel with trepidation, half expecting her to burst out laughing, or to say, *Here? You came here? To the ER? That cut doesn't even need Band-Aids.* But she doesn't. She holds my arm very gently in her (slightly sweaty) hands and squeezes it back together with her thumbs.

"You've just nicked the top of an artery there. You're very lucky. A little deeper and you could have . . ." I could have what? Died? "It could have been a lot worse."

I look at the nurse's name badge: MILLIE, NURSE, EMER-GENCY DEPT. Outside my cubicle, some paramedics wheel in a middle-aged man still in his suit. I wonder vaguely what his job is. Banker? Lawyer? Travel agent?

"Well, I think it will close up nicely."

In the cubicle next to me, the machine that the banker/lawyer/travel agent has been rigged up to is beeping. Beep. Beep. I hear someone talking to him.

"Hello, John? I'm Matthew, one of the ER doctors. Do you have any pain?"

The man named John grunts in reply.

"OK—have you had any pain relief? No? In that case, we're going to give you some acetaminophen. It will help with that, all right?"

Beep. Beep.

Millie returns with a tray of dressings and a tube of what I recognize to be saline solution.

"Can I just check your blood pressure?" I offer my arm and she slips the cuff on. As it squeezes, my scars become dark and my cut begins to bleed more heavily. "Oh, sorry. I should've done it on the other arm . . ."

Beep. Beep.

"John, we need to take some blood and insert a cannula." John makes another incoherent sound. "No, it's just a sharp scratch. The cannula is in case we need to put a line in."

Matthew is dressed all in dark blue and is carrying a pink stethoscope. He appears from the cubicle next door, drawing the curtains, walking purposefully past my cubicle.

Beep. Beep.

Millie washes the cut with the entire tube of saline solution, dabs it dry.

"You haven't done anything silly with pills, have you?" she asks, looking up at me, daring me to lie. She turns to Emma, who also shakes her head. "I saw your notes . . ."

"No," I reply quietly, "not this time."

She says nothing but starts to fill a syringe with anesthetic. "This will sting a little," she says. I wince and turn away from the throbbing hole in my arm. "You OK?" I nod curtly. She starts to put me back together with thick blue thread and a hooked needle slipping through my skin.

"Can you give me your arm, John? Can I roll up your sleeves?"

Beep. Beep.

My arm throbs.

"I'm just going to tie this around your arm. It's a bit tight."

Millie tugs in another stitch.

"You've got some good veins, John, this will be easy."

"How many more?" I ask, battling the urge to yank away my arm.

Beep. Beep.

"Maybe nine or ten," Millie says. "Not long."

I notice a tattoo of a butterfly on the top of her arm.

"OK now, sharp scratch." John groans.

I can almost see it, the needle slipping through the skin,

Matthew untying the rubber strip, filling up the tubes, inserting the cannula, probably making a mess. Doctors always make a mess.

Three stitches down. A thin trickle of blood worms out of the cut, down the curve of my arm.

Beep. Beep.

"There we go, John. We should get the results back in a couple of hours. Is there anything else that I can do for you?" More moaning. "I'll just sit you up, shall I?" The creaking of the mattress being bent into a ninety-degree angle. "Do you want your curtains open or shut?" No response. "I'll leave them open, so you can see what's going on. It's less boring that way." Matthew reappears with a tray, disappears into a room opposite.

Beep. Beep.

Millie dresses my arm with gauze and tape, and Emma rings for a taxi back to the unit. We stand outside the hospital next to an old man smoking his life away. I want a cigarette. Twelve stitches sitting in my arm. Snaking up to my elbow.

I am watched all night. Back to square one.

Dr. Flores takes me off one-on-one the following morning. *Obviously he can't be bothered with me anymore.* Thoughts muddle their way into my brain like angry strokes of graffiti. Everything is muffled by the flat ache of failure. I am a three-time failure.

My arm is swollen and bruised, the skin around my stitches sore and puckered with shades of purple and gray, but it is back together and if not for the stiff wad of dressings along my arm, I could pretend nothing has happened.

They searched my bedroom and have stolen every single blood-encrusted blade I've hidden—among balls of Blu Tack on my noticeboard, swimming in a bottle of foundation, between the pages of my history textbook. They found them all. They've taken most of my clothes, too, but by the time they'd taken my socks I'd started to think it was a little petty.

Elle doesn't talk to me at breakfast. She focuses on placing slices of bread in the toaster in the kitchen with a nurse, who watches her carefully in case she tries to electrocute herself or something. She sits at the other end of the table from where she usually sits, closer to the door. Jasper argues about eating his cereal, so eventually he is allowed to eat it with a plastic teaspoon. I guess it feels like less food in his mouth. Patient Will complains that his room has been rigged with cameras again; he's felt the electronic waves. Lopsided Nurse hasn't rubbed in her foundation so there's a shadowy line around her chin, and she's tried a new shade of nude lip gloss that doesn't work with her heavy mascara.

There is a lot of noise in my brain this morning, did I say that? Like a fuzzy old-fashioned television, the sort that used to crackle with static electricity when they got hot. That is my brain, just louder. I start a bowl of Fruit 'N Fibre, but I don't taste anything, so I swap halfway through to a piece of toast that Elle has made. I spread Marmite like it's peanut butter, layers and layers of thick, gloopy paste, because I need something to feel. Even if it is just the overwhelming sting of yeast extract.

Dr. Flores saunters into the dining room and beckons to me, and, defeated by the toast, I jump straight up and follow him. His trousers gather an inch above his ankles today, and he fumbles with his waistcoat as he ushers me into his office with a manner of over-practiced soothing.

He sits down and swirls milk into his coffee.

"How are you feeling, on a sca—"

"Zero," I reply dully.

He taps the NHS teaspoon against the NHS mug. "Really?"

"Zero," I say again adamantly.

"How is your arm feeling?"

I shrug.

He shrugs back. "Uncomfortable, I'd imagine."

"Yeah. It's about an eight."

He smiles. "Took the words right out of my mouth. So"— he takes a sip of coffee—"why did you . . . ?" He makes a slicing action along his arms and I wince.

"Don't do that."

He doesn't apologize. "How can we help you, Tamar?"

"You're the doctor."

He nods. "You're right, I am. I can give a diagnosis, I can prescribe medication, but I can't—"

"What's wrong with me, then?" I say. "You tell everyone else what's wrong with them—Jasper's anorexic, Elle's bipolar. What am I? Or am I just making all this up to waste your time?"

I think he takes that as a threat. It isn't meant to be.

He stirs the mug of coffee. "You know, Tamar, sometimes labels aren't the most helpful thing. Eating disorders are clear. Sectioned patients are required to have a diagnosis. You've got some problems, and that's why you're here; we're here to help you work through them."

I'm still waiting for the day that Dr. Flores says something that isn't a quotation pulled hastily from a textbook.

"What can I do to help you?"

I watch him as closely as he watches me, and feel a twinge of pride when his eyes lower first.

"You can't," I respond flatly. "And I think labels are helpful."

"That's very useful to know," he says.

It isn't useful to know. He doesn't want my opinion on his opinions. I notice he isn't wearing hair gel today, but I can't work out whether it makes him look better or worse. Less like a hedgehog, at least.

"Do you want to talk about last night?" he ventures again.

"There's nothing you don't know already," I say.

"Yes, but I'd like to hear it from you, so I can get a better picture, and we can have a think about where to go from here."

"I guess I messed up a bit, I wasn't thinking."

"You weren't trying to kill yourself?" he says.

"No, I just took it a bit far. It was an accident." I'm quite a good liar—have I mentioned that before?

"So, you're not feeling suicidal? What's the risk of it happening again?"

I don't tell him that the desire for death has been raging through my veins like a stampede of angry bulls, and that every fiber of my disgusting being should be charred and powdered in a dusty crematorium.

"I'm OK," I say. "It was just a slipup, I'm sorry."

"Don't be sorry, Tamar. I'm really glad we've been able to have this chat today. I think what I'm going to do is keep you in the unit this weekend, just to let things settle. Is that all right?"

"Yeah, whatever," I say. I don't care, I don't care whether I stay in the unit forever. It doesn't matter where I am. Nothing matters, really.

"How do you think the risperidone is going?"

"It doesn't stabilize my mood, it just makes me tired. And I drool at night," I reply. "Elle said it can shrink your brain."

Dr. Flores waves his hand dismissively and laughs. "Don't listen to Elle—I haven't heard anything like that. We'll leave it as it is at the moment, and maybe we can think about increasing it later on. The side effects should lessen with time, too."

"OK," I say. "That's fine, I don't mind."

"Can you tell me what's been bothering you these past few days? You've been seeming quite unsettled to some of the staff, would you agree with that?"

"Yeah, I suppose."

"Why?"

Why? I can ponder that question in my sedated brain for days and I still won't have any answers. It's hard to make space for other thoughts when you only want to kill yourself. In fact, it's hard to make space for anything. It's hard to make space for remembering to eat or piss or smile when it's expected of you. I answer him, though, and that surprises me.

"It's just Iris. Yesterday was her birthday."

"Ah. How old would she have been?"

"Seventeen," I say. My mouth has been hijacked and the words are spilling out like the tumbling water in the dam where she died. I don't talk about Iris, and no one talks to me about her. Except Mia. That is how it was. But now . . .

"I see. How does that make you feel? Thinking about her?"

"Like crap," I say. "I hate it." I can feel a pulse in my thumb.

"Why?" he says. "What is it that makes you feel like crap? Do you think it's your fault?"

I know she is dead. I know that Iris is dead. I know that it was sudden and so shocking that the waves of horror shimmered in the distance for months afterward. I also know that it is my fault, that one second she was there and her heart pumped crimson blood through her veins, and the next she was gone, blood frozen solid, and I could have prevented it, but I did not.

"It wasn't your fault, what happened with Iris, you understand that, don't you?" he ventures, leaning apprehensively toward me. "Can you tell me what happened?"

My mind darts through the maze of lies, trying to find the truth tangled in its prickly boundaries.

"I don't talk about Iris," I say.

He ignores me. "When you were lying in the bath, were you thinking about her?"

"I always think about her." Iris is the unfitting piece of the jigsaw in my brain. Of course I was thinking about her in the bath. How could I not?

"What were you thinking?" he says.

"That the bathwater was probably a lot warmer than the river." That is a lie. I wasn't thinking that.

But the truth always gets you in the end.

"Really?" says Dr. Flores with a tone of skepticism. He likes to think he can see through my lies.

"I didn't want her to die," I say suddenly.

"I know, Tamar. I don't think anyone wanted her to die. Sometimes terrible things just happen."

He's wrong, because it didn't "just happen." It wasn't a fluke or an accident. It happened because of me.

"No, it wasn't like that," I splutter. "I really didn't want her to die; it was all a mistake."

"No one wanted her to die, Tamar. These things just happen, unfortunately." He's repeating himself.

Dr. Flores looks at me inquiringly. I look at the floor beneath him, where his suede-clad feet shuffle slightly. Then

I look at the squeaky wheels on his chair, the way Post-it notes and string spill out of the drawers in his desk. I don't look at him.

"Things don't 'just happen,'" I say softly. "It didn't 'just happen.' It's my fault."

"Often, Tamar, when people die in this way, in the way that Iris died, it can feel very sudden and scary, and people blame themselves when it really isn't their fault at all; it's a very common response. But that doesn't make it your fault."

"Shut up! Stop saying it isn't my fault!"

It's all just white noise, whirs and cogwheels turning in my brain, a treadmill of buzzes and bangs spiraling in the air and into my pounding eardrums. No, no, no. Nothing but fog and the muffled sounds of I don't know what.

"Why is it your fault, Tamar?"

Why am I not dead yet?

"Tell me about Iris."

"I can't talk about Iris! Stop talking about Iris . . . It *is* my fault, you know fuck all!"

I'm staring blankly at the equally blank walls of the recovery room, slow and stupid and dosed up on some medication that I can't remember taking. I think I'm on five-minute observations; I can hear someone lifting and shutting the viewing slat fairly often, but I don't turn to look at the face peering through. It's too much effort. My neck hurts.

The "recovery room" is a euphemism; it's a room with nothing in it at all—just four white walls, the kind of room they warn you about in films. Four whitewashed walls and a patient in a drug-induced stupor. Nothing else, not even a bed. It's cold—there are no windows, so they've overcompensated with the air conditioning. The fact that I'm in here means I've done something shitty. I just can't remember what. My hands are clasped tightly together like I've been scheming, my fingers streaked with red where I must've been squeezing them too tightly.

After a while, Emma comes in with a cup of tea with milk and two sugars, as always.

"It's sweet," I say as I take a sip even though it's too hot. My voice is hoarse, like I've been shouting a lot.

"Oh, I put in three sugars this time. You looked like you needed a sugar boost. Milk and three sugars, sorry." She sits down, cross-legged, on the floor with me, turns her clipboard upside down so I can't read her notes.

"How are you feeling?" she says.

"Like I've been whacked over the head with a hammer," I say, and she smiles.

"It's probably the lorazepam. It can make you tired."

"I know. What did I do?"

"When?" She falters.

"To get myself in here," I say. "What happened?"

"Can you not remember?"

I shake my head.

I'd stood up in Dr. Flores's office, she tells me, shouting and swearing every swear word in the English language. I'd headed to his bookcase and hurled the books with the hardest covers I could find at him. He'd swerved just as the Holy Bible smashed into his computer. He didn't have his emergency alarm with him so he just had to yell like a child for someone to come. It took twenty long seconds for three nurses to arrive, crumbs still on their lips from the cake they'd had to leave in the nursing office. They'd pinned me against the wall closest to the bookshelf and, according to Emma, I'd tried to bite them as they held my squirming body with sticky-icing fingers. I think I must have bitten the insides of my cheeks instead, because they feel flayed and a metallic taste lingers in my mouth. I don't like the tea but I drink it anyway to rinse away the taste of blood. I have finger marks on my wrists and bruises peppered around my collarbone.

"Are you feeling well enough for dinner?" she asks. "They're nearly finished but I can get you a sandwich."

My head spins like a Catherine wheel as I pull myself up to standing. "I can come," I say.

Neither of us mentions Iris.

THEN

A new year. Toby stubbed out his half-finished cigarette and squashed it into the pavement as he leaned forward to hug me. He was wearing his school uniform.

"You all right?" he asked, slipping a Polo into his mouth, because if anything could hide the stench of stale smoke, it was mints. "I saw you in the corridor at school today, but I didn't have time to come over and see you, my business coursework was due in."

"Don't worry," I said. "I didn't stay long, anyway."

"I know you didn't, you never stay long!"

"I'd rather sleep." It wasn't a lie. If I could spend every second of my life asleep until the day I died, wouldn't everything be infinitely easier?

Toby took another Polo from the packet. "Chips and vinegar?"

"Chips and no vinegar," I said.

"Half and half?"

"Fine, then, but you're paying."

It was one pound per paper bag of chips, seeping with grease, and we ate them on the pavement outside the takeaway, the smell diffusing into my hair so that it became the scent of Herbal Essences deep-fried and battered. Two homeless men with a scraggly-looking greyhound asked for four pounds for a pack of chips each. Toby told them they were a pound a bag and gave them two pounds. They fist-bumped him and walked straight past the takeaway and into the supermarket at the end of the road.

"Chips," he snorted. "As if. More like a can of Budweiser and a packet of Royals."

"How's Mia?" I asked. I asked this every time we saw each other, and his answers were always vague and uncomfortable. I was waiting for the day that he'd say, "Oh, Mia? She's great, she wants to be friends again. She's really sorry." It was never going to happen, I knew that. "She's fine," he said. "Yeah, she's good." He awkwardly pulled out his packet of cigarettes and was suddenly engrossed in lighting one.

"Good," I said. "I'm glad."

"Got any New Year's resolutions, then?" said Toby, making no secret of the fact that he was trying to change the subject. "Going to give up smoking?"

I laughed. "Not this year; I've done that one enough." I'd given up smoking "for real this time" at the dawn of each New Year for three years now.

I did have a New Year's resolution. It just wasn't the sort you brought up in polite conversation. Or impolite conversation, for that matter.

"How about you?"

"No, I've got nothing, either. I thought about the whole

giving up chocolate thing, but, really, what is the point? I like it, so I'll eat it. I'm not denying myself a bar of Cadbury's just because. There needs to be actual meaning behind it."

There was meaning behind mine. Check.

"Yeah, I think the whole thing's a bit stupid, to be honest. It's just another day," I said. He dived his hand into the crumpled bag and finished the last chip.

"You're such a cynic," he said, between mouthfuls of starch. "I think this year's going to be amazing."

Amazing? I thought back to my New Year's resolution, scrawled in black ink on the pages of my diary. I thought of that whole diary entry, dated December 31, the vitriol and the venom seeping through the pages in the words that I had written to myself, smudged with the tears that had pounded onto the paper. I didn't want to make it through another year. I didn't deserve to, not when the girl I had killed was decaying and moldy in her grave. So, in some ways, my New Year's resolution was amazing, I guess. It was fitting, at least. It was necessary. I was going to be dead.

When I woke up on the day that I was going to kill myself, I expected to feel something, but there was nothing, bar a slight gnawing in my stomach that I took to be fear. I was as cold and as calculating as the day that I had murdered Iris. The weather, too. I'd hoped for thunderstorms and lightning bolts ricocheting from Olympus, or lemonade-slurping, sun-drenched skies, but got neither. It was cool, gray, and unspectacular. In fact, there was nothing to mark it out as a special day at all, but for the small x in my diary next to January 7.

I got up and made myself breakfast, like I would on a normal day. Brew thumped his tail as I came down the stairs. My parents were out at work and I'd planned it that way, so it was just me, Brew, and the plate of scrambled eggs on the kitchen counter. I didn't know why I'd made scrambled eggs—I'd never made them before.

I watched two hours of daytime television, because I could, because there was no point in rushing things. I had time. Brew sat at my feet. I didn't check my phone. Not once. There was no point. Jeremy Kyle shouted at a platinum-blonde teenage mother. I switched the TV off. I was supposed to go to school that afternoon for a history lesson. Fat chance.

I tried not to think back over every terrible thing I'd ever done, because I was meant to be feeling relieved, but I couldn't help myself. It was the last time I'd be able to think, ever again. May as well make the most of it.

I ran a bath in the old bathroom, the one I didn't use anymore, the one with stickers of dolphins and mermaids trawling the tiles on the walls. I sloshed the water around with my hands to make the temperature even. Having a bath was important, for some reason. My dead body needed to be clean. Clean and submerged, like a body in a river.

I held a green bath bomb that smelled of chamomile and claimed to be packed with deep-sea minerals in my hands, but I didn't put it in. I forgot, I think.

I slipped into the bath. The mermaids on the walls moved. Plunging below the surface, water burning nostrils, dancing into lungs that in equal measure try to accept and reject in confusion the muddy flood that prances into them. Water stomping and head banging about quivering eyelids, each slap more animated than the last. No breath. Flailing arms and spluttering and booming in pounding ears. Tiny milliseconds of air smacking against bleeding lips. And the water dances, pirouettes, more crazed than ever, cackling in delight, wildly spinning in ecstasy, anticipating the drowning. And my lungs are swamped by something more overwhelming than the water itself. Fear charges through my spasming nerves and swallows my sinking brain, and fear wins, right up until the water dance is over and my body is so dead that it doesn't even feel itself as it is hurled against the rocky pit of the dam, cracking like a clay pigeon splintering against a bullet.

I gasped for air as I emerged from the floor of the bathtub, the bitter taste of soapy water lingering on my tongue. My ears fizzed like they had been filled with popping candy. The bathwater was cold. I might have been in there for two, three hours, maybe more, I didn't know. But I knew that I was being crushed by something, the heaviness of the air pressing down against my chest and my stomach. I was alive, and painfully aware of every breath I took, every ripple on the surface of the water as my icy fingers twitched. Cracked crimson nail polish. The water had turned a pale pink where the color from my hair had run. Outside, it was starting to get dark as the day waned and the clock ticked and I was still alive.

You've already murdered one person, it won't be difficult to do it again.

I stood up from the bath but didn't feel a change in temperature. Everything was cold.

There was a curtain rail in the bedroom and shoelaces in the shoes under the radiator. I polished the shoes because it seemed like the right thing to do and I turned small packets of chalky pills over in my hands but afterward couldn't remember if I had swallowed them all. I practiced knots and nooses on the floor of the bedroom over and over, until I was as good as a sailor; as good as the very water dwellers themselves. Then I wondered if it hurt to die but Google could not tell me the answer. I wondered if it hurt to drown. I wondered about heaven and hell and reincarnation. I wondered if now was the time to repent my sins, and would that help anything? Would begging for forgiveness help anything? I wondered a lot of things on the floor of the bedroom, but it didn't help, because I was still alive. I was still alive.

I can't remember the expression on my dad's face. Can't remember why he had come home early or whether he was still wearing his tie or if he'd taken it off, like he usually did. I can't remember what he said, how he said it, or if he said anything at all.

But I can remember that he did not approach. Did not hold my shaking body or my cracked-crimson fingertips, or wipe the saliva from my chin. He left that to the paramedics, who took me with blue flashing lights in a too-hot ambulance to the hospital and sat with me and brought me blankets when my dad did not. I can remember that my dad did not want to see his precious daughter crumpled on the floor with shoelaces around her neck, and that he turned away from the broken curtain rail and clumps of wall plaster before him, and he kicked the bedroom door so hard that the whole room shuddered for minutes afterward.

"There haven't been any self-harm incidents for a week now."

"Oh, good," says my mum. "I'm so glad to hear that."

There are four of us in Therapy Room 1, crammed around a small table that the nurses have dragged in from their office: Dr. Flores, Nurse Will, my mum, and me. My mind is wandering. Like I thought that first day, it is stupid to call it Therapy Room 1; it's the only "therapy room" in the whole building. No one here has therapy, anyway.

"It is," agrees Dr. Flores. "On the other hand, we're not thinking about discharge just yet. After her . . . *erratic* behavior on Friday, I think Tamar would concur that we really need to have a little more time to assess what's going on."

Friday. I still don't remember my "erratic behavior."

"OK," says Mum, but I can see she's disappointed. "How much longer, do you think?"

I think she is desperate to pull me out of the false environment that I've been living in and back into the fear and bewilderment and pain of real life.

Dr. Flores pauses. "Let's think in weeks, rather than months, shall we?" Weeks makes it sound shorter. "We're carrying on with the risperidone," he continues. "The side effects should continue to wear off over the next week or so, but if they don't, there are other options."

Two little oval pills: one in the morning, one in the evening.

My mum remains quiet and contemplative, as if there isn't much left for her to fight for, or maybe there is so much that it is utterly overwhelming. She nods in a way that every psychiatrist would love their clients to: Yes, you're right. You know our daughter better than we do, congratulations.

"As far as home leave is concerned, we're going to give her a night at home soon and see how things go from there."

There is a lot of guesswork. A lot of "just see what happens." You never know, she might not kill herself—wouldn't that be nice? I am supposed to go home, spend a night in my own house, my own bedroom, my own bed with its polka-dot duvet. I can eat what I want, when I want it, and drink as many cups of green tea as I like. I'll have to negotiate the tangles of my mind, though, in the blackness of the night, ignore the twisted messages that my brain sends, ricocheting through my nerves.

"Brilliant," says Mum, her cheeks lifting into a smile. Is she secretly as nervous as me?

"I want you to imagine you are a tree. Would you be an oak, tall and strong, or perhaps the long-lived chestnut tree?"

Elle rolls her eyes at me. It is four in the afternoon, and everyone has been crammed into Therapy Room 1 with its headache-inducing pink, given stuffing-less beanbag chairs to sit on, and told to get on with it.

Janice, the occupational therapist, often says that she likes to "explore through play," but she also seems to forget what she is supposed to be exploring a lot of the time, or that play is supposed to be fun. She's given us a piece of paper each and is waiting with a childish expression on her face for us to draw a tree of our choice.

"Jasper, would you mind sharing with the group what tree you've chosen?"

Jasper awkwardly holds up a messy drawing. "Apple," he says.

"And why have you chosen an apple tree, Jasper?"

"I like apples." He shrugs, and Elle snorts from our corner.

"How about Will?"

Patient Will looks up from his beanbag chair cocoon, holding the piece of paper. "Sorry, I just made an airplane . . ."

he says, and attempts to hurl it across the room. It lands at his feet.

Janice sits up in her chair, looking disgruntled. "Well, how about you have a think now, and we'll come back to you?"

"OK, great," he replies enthusiastically.

Janice doesn't notice the sarcasm, or if she does, she ignores it and chooses to twiddle the rings on her fingers instead.

"I'll go next, then," she says brightly. "I've drawn an aspen tree, which symbolizes the overcoming of fears and the determination that lives inside us all."

"It's just a tree, though," cuts in Elle bluntly. "I mean, I wouldn't want to *be* a tree. They don't do anything, they just sit there for hundreds and hundreds of years until they die. I don't see the fun in that."

"Yes, but this exercise isn't about that, it's about exploring—"

"Trees?" Elle says skeptically.

Janice clumsily adjusts a pin in her dreadlocks. "How about you, Harper, what have you drawn?"

"A palm tree."

"Excellent! What is it about a palm tree that appeals to you?"

"Don't know. Can't draw any other trees, really. I guess they're quite cool . . ." She trails off, as if suddenly aware of the faces staring at her.

"They are cool," says Janice. "Let's have a think about palm trees, shall we?"

She's clutching at straws here; even Harper doesn't have anything to say about palm trees, and she's drawn one. Elle lets out a very audible groan and nudges me. Janice ignores her.

"What are some qualities of a palm tree?"

"They're easy to draw," says Elle sardonically. Jasper laughs from the other side of the room.

"Anything else? They're usually found in hot places, aren't they?" Janice announces, as if waiting for us to suddenly fall happily onto her wavelength. No one speaks.

"Well, they could be the bearer of shade from harsh sunlight. Or perhaps they are a ray of hope on a lonely desert island. How can we apply this to our own lives? Perhaps

Harper chose a palm tree because she would be a good shoulder to cry on when things get hard?"

"Oh, for fuck's sake," says Elle. "She told you why she drew a palm tree; this has got nothing to do with anything."

"Elle, if you're going to disturb the balance of this group, then I'm afraid I'm going to have to ask you to leave."

"That's fine, I'm going. This is a total waste of time."

Janice watches her as she sweeps out, a bemused and slightly crestfallen expression on her face, as if she can't quite work out why nobody else seems to love analyzing trees as much as she does. I can't help but feel a twinge of sympathy for her. She sits there, quiet and motionless for a few seconds, before sitting up straight and brightly continuing as if nothing has happened. We could all learn something from palm trees, you see.

Once we are allowed to leave, twenty minutes later, I find Elle in the dining room, animatedly playing chess with Nurse Will.

"Check," she announces as I walk in, flamboyantly slamming a rook down on the board.

"No," says Nurse Will exasperatedly. "You can't move diagonally with a rook, I just told you. You have to move straight."

"*Your* rooks might have to move straight," she responds shortly, knocking his bishop from his square. It rolls off the table and onto the floor.

"Charming," he says with a smirk. "Look, Elle, we can't play if you're not following the rules."

"Who makes the rules, though?" says Elle. "Why can't I make them? I'd make much better rules than whoever made these ones."

I sigh and sit down at the other end of the room, busy myself with a crossword that I can't solve. I can't be bothered with Elle when she is like this—when she's snappy and agitated and too sure of her own abilities to conquer the world and every other universe besides. It's exhausting.

And she gets so confused. She told me she could fly once, and three members of staff had to hold her back from the stairwell. Then she said she was being discharged and sat by the air-locked doors for hours, her packed suitcase next to her. Once she forgot she needed to use the toilet because she was too busy telling the world about the time she'd created her own star in the universe. She blushed when she saw the damp stain on the beanbag chair.

Dr. Flores sweeps into the room. His glasses are askew on his nose and he holds his phone in his hand, covering the mouthpiece.

"Elle, can I borrow you a minute?" he says quietly, with a wave of his free hand.

"I'm playing chess," she says dismissively.

"Don't worry, it can wait," says Nurse Will. "You should see Dr. Flores now."

"Fine, then, but don't change the board while I'm gone," says Elle, darting toward the door that Dr. Flores holds open for her with his foot.

Nurse Will snorts. "As if," he says.

I catch up with her an hour later as she sidles out of the bathroom, hurriedly wiping mascara off her cheeks.

"Dr. Flores has refused to write me up leave, like he said he would if I was doing well," she mutters gloomily as she shuts the door to my bedroom, "because my foster parents aren't having me back. They said they 'can't handle me,' so I've got nowhere to live. Again."

"What?" I say, even though I've heard her perfectly.

"They were long-term, as well," she continues. "I was supposed to live with them until I turned eighteen and got a place of my own, but I figured they'd still let me come back for Christmas and stuff, you know. I've lived with them for over three years and now they're just throwing me out like a piece of crap."

"Elle . . ." I say, because I don't know what I should say. I think of my mum and dad, who've stuck by me like barnacles through everything, even though I didn't want them to. Elle has never had that; from the moment her mother overdosed on heroin in front of her when she was three, she hasn't had that. That's her first memory.

"I'm so stupid, I'm so stupid," she groans, collapsing onto my pillow and tossing her hair in front of her tear-filled eyes.

"You're not stupid, Elle," I say awkwardly. "You're not."

"I am, though. I thought they were more than just foster parents. They were my family, and even they don't want me. Now I have no one all over again."

The spark in her voice is missing. She speaks in a flat monotone without pausing for breath and she sits, hunched over, like she's been punched heavily in the stomach, wiping her face with a grubby sleeve.

"You have me," I say, sitting down beside her and pulling back her sheet of ginger hair.

"Thanks," she says, her voice muffled by her blocked nose. "I really thought I meant something to them, you know? But I didn't, they hated me all along. I'm so stupid," she repeats, triggering another wave of tears spilling down her freckled cheeks and soaking into the fabric of the pillow. I've never seen her so small.

"It's not your fault . . ."

"It is my fault. There must be something wrong with me.

I've gone through ten different foster families. You know my name: Elle Simon? Where's the Simon from? I don't even know. Was it my mum's name? I don't know anything. I'm a nobody."

"Elle . . ."

"This is all so pointless," she says, ignoring me. "I'm never going to get out now, even if I am trying, because I've got nowhere to go. And I *have* been trying. I need to get out of here; I hate it, I hate being locked up; I only asked for a night."

"Is there nowhere else you can stay, just for the night?" I ask unhelpfully.

Elle throws me a look of contempt. "What, like the delightful hostel I stayed at when I was twelve? Great idea, Tay."

"Sorry," I say, stung. "I really am sorry, Elle."

"I know. Me, too," she mumbles, her chest rising and falling quickly with her uneven breaths. "I'm sorry, too."

Screeching.

Who's dying? Slapped into consciousness by the relentless wails of the emergency alarm. Adrenaline pumping. Someone is screaming. Nurses in blue sprinting past the window slats in my bedroom door. I turn over in bed and try to imagine that the day has not begun with someone trying to kill themselves. The alarm continues to shriek.

Thump.

It's not Elle, I tell myself. Let's call her Distressed Patient A . . .

I imagine sweaty hands restraining Distressed Patient A on the floor as she squirms and spits like an animal.

Snip.

Slicing off the ligature spun from pieces of knitted wool stolen from art group.

Distressed Patient A swears like a human five times.

Nurse Will tries to talk sense into the fragmented mind of Distressed Patient A as she continues to yell louder than the alarm, face pressed sideways against the itchy carpet.

I close my eyes.

Doors opening.

"Get back into your room."

Doors slamming.

Distressed Patient A prays to God for it all to end, fractured cries between weeping. God doesn't hear.

The alarm ceases, and the corridors are bathed in a blissful silence, broken only by the defeated snivels coming from next door as Distressed Patient A solemnly accepts a dose of diazepam in a paper cup. My clock on my bedside beeps: 7 a.m.

Nurse Will strides into my bedroom without knocking and sweeps open the flimsy curtains, which makes no difference as they already let in the light. It is raining.

"Rise and shine, lazybones, it's a lovely day." As if I haven't heard the commotion.

I can still hear Distressed Patient A crying softly.

I'm on leave. At home, but at a party. It's Toby's house, his party, and the room is heaving full of sober people pretending to have a good time. It is a high-heeled, tight-little-black-dress-with-slits-down-the-back affair. Bottles of cider in hands, waiting for the sweetened taste of Bulmers and for tipsy to kick in. No one notices me sitting in an armchair in the corner, the unpleasant presence lingering like the stain on the living room carpet. I don't mind. I said I don't like being noticed already, I think. Boys from the year above play spin the bottle in the dim, unlit side of the room, swearing brazenly and filming exaggeratedly passionate kisses on their phones for permanent humiliation. The smell of body sweat permeates the air. Crushed Doritos underfoot.

"Tamar!" Toby walks into the room and sidles his way through the near-impenetrable sea of people. "I'm so glad you came." He sits down on the floor near the armchair. We smile awkwardly at each other, pretending not to remember the fiasco of the last time I saw him.

"How are things?" I say, slipping onto the floor to join him.

"Good, yeah. Are you doing all right?"

"I guess, yeah. Depends what you mean by 'all right.' If

trying to kill your psychiatrist is all right, then, yeah, I'm brilliant."

He laughs. I wish I was joking.

"I really have missed you," he says earnestly. "When you're discharged, we should hang out more, go into town and get chips, for old times' sake, or something."

"What about Mia?" I say. He shrugs.

"She doesn't have to come. She can look after herself. Look, I am really sorry about it . . . at the hospital . . . I heard. I wouldn't have brought her . . ." He trails off.

"How is she?"

"Same as ever, really . . . Still hates your guts, you know, the normal stuff," he says with a grin. "Angry with me for siding with you after the hospital, so I've got no smoking buddies. It's kind of lonely." He laughs, and I can see him reliving that day. I sigh. "You drinking?"

"I don't know. I said I wouldn't," I say half-heartedly, even though I know now that I am going to be drinking. Now that Toby has offered me the magic elixir to cure my nerves.

"Just have a shot or two's worth," Toby says. "Your mum won't even notice. You may as well make the most of your freedom . . ."

If anyone asks, it is the peer pressure that means I have one shot, then drink the rest of the bottle single-handedly, like it is water, on the kitchen floor, until the room swirls and Toby's face turns to Plasticine before my eyes. The room is revolving around me, darkly dressed people shouting in my ears and brushing against my back, a smashed bottle of WKD spilled on the floor, its blue stain leaching into the tiles. I think the laughter comes from me, an explosion about the hilarity of the whole damn world, because I've managed to forget how amusing it is. I'm still laughing as I exclaim, "I'm not drunk at all, I can still walk in a straight line, look," and hurtle headfirst into the front door just as someone swings it open, my forehead meeting the door with a crack. Unamused hands of sober people hoist me up and sit me in a chair with water in a plastic cup so it won't matter if I drop it. Toby is speaking to me, but I'm not listening to what he is saying because I am more interested in the unusual shade of his eyes; they're grayer than I've noticed before, and flecked with tiny specks of peacock green that you can't see unless you're close up.

Then there is Toby and there is me in a room full of people and I feel his face up close to mine even though my vodka-brain is swirling my vision and Rihanna bursts on, but it is just background noise. I brush my lips against his and I don't think it lasts for more than a few seconds.

"Sorry," I mumble awkwardly, drawing my arms away from his back.

"It's OK," he says, still leaning toward me.

"No, it's not. I'm drunk . . ." I laugh.

"Yeah, you are. We'll talk about it in the morning . . ."

Fast-forward to the morning, the morning in question.

I wake up in my bed and vomit clings to my hair in solid, plaster-like lumps. I'm covered in four duvets and the radiator is on high but I am strangely cold. I've got a horrible taste in my mouth. I get out of bed and to my surprise find myself promptly crashing straight into my chest of drawers and collapsing on the floor. Bit strange. Then I see EKG stickers on my wrists and chest, and I remember that I went to a party. Shit, what the hell happened last night? I stagger to the bathroom and attempt to wash with water that feels far too hot on my fingers but at best lukewarm against my face. And with each splash the pieces of last night start to come together like a broken jigsaw puzzle.

I was at Toby's house party. He'd invited me an hour before it started, and Mia wasn't there. Vodka was there, though. And the rest, I have no idea. I stumble back into my room and lie down because I can feel a throbbing headache coming on. I don't know where my mum is. I know that Dad is at work.

As the morning wears by, my hangover begins to wane and I stagger into the shower and hold myself steady against the temperature switches. The place on my arm where my stitches are stings as shampoo slithers into the scab.

"Tamar? Come out, I need to talk to you." Mum looks more hungover than me. She's scowling.

Oh shit.

"You said you weren't going to drink at this party, it was the one condition, so what's this? How are we going to explain to Dr. Flores the fact that four hours after you arrive home you end up in the back of an ambulance because you don't know your own limits? How's that going to make us look?"

"I don't know. I just got . . . It was an accident," I say lamely.

"An accident?!" she splutters. "Please do tell me how throwing vodka down your own throat is an accident. I would love to know."

"Look, I've got a splitting headache, can we just leave it . . ."

I try to make a smoothie from avocado and mint and kiwi fruit in a vague attempt to be healthy, as if this will combat the unhappiness my liver went through last night, but it is disgusting. Clearly, health and happiness aren't for me. I eat half a jar of Nutella with a spoon instead.

Brew comes into the room, his chocolate tail wagging during a slobbery greeting. He leans his head against my knees, panting, his tongue lolling out over his gray muzzle.

My dad came up with the name Brew. I think he was referencing beer, but I'm not sure; I was only eight when we brought him home, age eight weeks. I sat with him on my lap in the back of the car, proudly sharing my seat belt by pulling it around his soft belly. He could fit in your pocket. Now he weighs thirty-one kilograms of solid Labrador and I can't pick him up if I try.

As I'm scooping the last of the Nutella out of the jar, fragments of last night start to piece together in my head.

I saw Toby, I remember, and he'd poured one shot of Sainsbury's Basics vodka into a shot glass shaped like a test tube, but I'd taken the bottle and helped myself. It tasted like paint stripper and it burned my throat like when you drink a cup of tea too quickly.

Then we'd kissed; I remember it in snapshots, like the film of an instant camera—the burnt taste of weed on his lips, although I'm not sure when or where he'd smoked it, the scent of cinnamon-flavored vodka as his hands brushed against my back, where my shoulder blades meet the middle of my spine.

"Shit," I say. I hope I've imagined it. I don't have any way of contacting him, either; my care plan clearly states that "Alice must not use her phone or the internet during home leave." No room for confusion at all. Alice, Tamar—there is hardly any difference. Lime Grove likes to make sure I am as far from normal as possible when I'm at home.

I'd vomited into the kitchen sink and onto the counters, that had happened. Doubled over and snorting vodka from my nose, with water in my eyes fuzzing over my already-blurred vision. There had been an ambulance, too, with its whirring lights and men in green, hence the EKG stickers, I suppose. There was nothing beyond that. I must have been well and truly gone.

I remember that brief second with Toby, though: It is the one lucid memory in a fog of nothing. When I think about it, it burns a hole in my stomach in the kind of way that only comes about once in a moon's cycle. I think it's a nice feeling, but I'm not sure, because I have been known to yearn for things that are not nice feelings. Ask Dr. Flores, and he'll tell you that I like to disconnect from my emotions. Apparently it's quite a pastime of mine.

I spend the day popping one painkiller too many at a time, to ward off the sharp headache that presses against my temples like a vice, hoping vaguely that Toby will turn up in shining armor and whisk me off to the one-pound chip shop. But he doesn't, and instead my mum takes me back to Lime Grove in the same old Vauxhall, just in time to be searched before evening group begins and we discuss how our day was.

"So . . . home leave, Tamar? I hear you went to a party," Dr. Flores says with a smug expression. We're in his office, but he smells of the tuna baguette he ate for lunch, awkwardly perched on the end of Ruby table, psychoanalyzing the way we eat mashed potatoes.

"Yeah. I did."

"Good party, was it? Ten out of ten?"

"I don't remember," I say bluntly. "I was too drunk."

He laughs. I'm surprised by his attitude. I expected a "Tamar is clearly a raging alcoholic; she must never be allowed to go to parties again."

"I'm pleased that you went. I'm not underestimating how difficult that must have been for you."

"Thanks," I mumble.

"Parties are difficult for most people at the best of times, so I really am very impressed."

Am I not "most people"? No, I guess not—I'm the margin of weird people crammed into the fringes of society.

"I made an idiot of myself," I say.

"Teenagers do that. They'll have forgotten about it in a week," he says with a dismissive wave of the hand.

He's wearing a new tie today. It has the structure of atoms swirled against a green background: electrons, protons, neutrons. It isn't as friendly as his periodic table one.

"So, you're not going to cancel leave next week?"

"Because of the party? No, of course not. I think you did

extremely well, all things considered. I heard you didn't self-harm."

"Were you expecting me to?"

He looks taken off guard. "Well—no, of course not, I mean . . ." he says, looking flustered. "The point is that you didn't, which you should celebrate."

Somebody whip out the party poppers.

"I didn't feel like it. What happens if I feel like it?"

"Well, I think you're not giving yourself enough credit, for starters. You could have self-harmed, but you didn't, which is admirable. Second, we need to start thinking of other things you can do in place of the self-harming."

Snap a rubber band. Hold an ice cube. Punch a pillow.

"Like what?" I say. "Painting my nails doesn't work."

"What about running?" says Dr. Flores.

I stopped running soon after Iris died. I was too slow, had started losing races. Not just missing out on the top three medal spots, but properly losing, bringing up the humiliated rear, wheezing and spluttering. Running was my thing: I couldn't lose. There was no point in doing it if it didn't end with a cold medal pressed against my chest. At first, Toby had tried to persuade me to come to training, but I knew they didn't need me. I was replaceable.

"What about it?" I say warily.

"Well, how about it?" he replies, crossing his legs purposefully.

"I don't run anymore," I say flatly. "I stopped."

"And that's exactly what I'm trying to say. How about next Saturday, you take yourself on a short run—ten minutes, say? Then on Monday, you can come back and tell us all how it went."

I know how it would go. I remember . . . I would stretch out on the path in the park, focusing on each area of my body from my toes up—hamstrings, thighs, shoulders—and then I would start running in the shoes that I hadn't worn for two years. They would be too stiff, hardened from the crusted hunks of mud that had dried onto them, and the backs would dig into my heels and make them bleed. I'd manage five minutes, maybe six, with the monster squatting heavier and heavier on my back, and then I wouldn't be able to run anymore. I wouldn't make ten minutes.

"Why, though?"

"Exercise is good," he says with a shrug. "It releases endorphins. It's an adaptive coping strategy."

Ah. He wants me to replace cold metal slitting my skin with a stitch in my abdomen.

"No one's saying you have to do competitions or anything, Tamar. We can make running something for you. The only person you need to better is yourself."

It isn't true, though, is it? I need to better every person around me ten times over before anyone will sit up and notice me. That's how the world works. What does he think exams and sports and Nobel Prizes are for?

"OK," I say. Whatever.

"I'm really glad that you're prepared to try. It will be good for you, I'm sure." He isn't sure. Psychiatrists are never sure, but they pretend to be. "Speaking of next weekend, how does trying the whole two nights at home sound to you?"

Terrifying. Nauseating. Overwhelming.

"Great," I say. "I'd love to go home for the whole weekend."

"I'm going to say that you're written up for two nights' leave, then, but I want you to ring up at any point if you're not coping. In fact," he says, pulling out his diary and scribbling a note, "I'll get someone on shift to give you a call on Saturday, just to check in . . ."

"Can I have my phone back?"

"I don't see why not," he says, with a smile that says, *God, teenagers!* "Maybe for an hour or so each day?"

"Sure," I say. "That's fine. Thanks." Cooperating is the key.

"Is there anything else you wanted to discuss?" he asks in a tone that indicates the conversation is very much over.

"Not really, no. Can I go?"

"By all means," he says.

The door is heavier to push than usual.

THEN

It's a funny thing, surviving after trying to murder yourself. An overwhelming blankness, an aching numbness enveloped me and ran deep into my bones. The too-hot ambulance dropped me off under layers of sweaty sheets in a too-hot hospital because January is the month of heating bills. They rigged me up to heart monitors and gave me a hospital gown with broken straps. Was I the victim? Or the perpetrator? Who was the person in the body lying on the hospital bed? I don't know. It wasn't me.

A fly buzzed feebly in the artificially white light above my head. Being toasted alive. Why are they attracted to light? I wondered if the fly was thinking that now: *Hmm, on second thought, maybe this wasn't such a good idea, now that I'm being frazzled.* Too late, buddy, too late. You're a goner.

When the vomiting began, I started to cry, and the fly stopped buzzing, which meant it was dead. But I was not dead. The poison in my veins made me vomit into the bowls and onto the bedsheets and into my hair and it would not stop. But I didn't care, because the pain coursed through me like I should be dead, no one could withstand this—my temples exploded and my esophagus burned. But with every retch I was reminded that I was so painfully alive. So very much a *failure.*

They pierced my gray skin with needles and rigged me up to a heart monitor and slipped a tube into my knuckle and a drip drip-dripped into my veins, but it did not stop the agony, because I was not dead. A nurse put a dressing on the friction burns around my neck.

"You'll be lovely and bruised in the morning," she said.

I was alone, because my parents could not bring themselves to look at my pathetic body contorted on a hospital bed, clinging onto the dear life that I did not want.

There was a toddler in the bed next to me who slept with raspy breaths, his mother on the chair next to him. A strange smell lingered in the air: musky sweat and scented bleach. The curtains in the pediatric ward were patterned with jungle animals—a failed attempt at giving the room personality. The air was thicker than honey, and my hair clung to my sweating forehead.

They gave me antidepressants, antipsychotics, mood stabilizers. Because that's all they could do. Other patients could talk for hours in their sweaty-palmed state about their *anxiety disorder*. The eating disorder patients, trapped in their unhealthy relationships with food, some of them emaciated, others not a pound off normal. The patients with such crippling depression that even getting out of bed in the morning was an achievement worthy of more than a pat on the back.

The monster that had swallowed me was different. The

experts soon exhausted their options: manic depression, schizophrenia, obsessive-compulsive disorder . . . But the monster didn't need a label or a name. The monster was me.

I stayed in the hospital for three days as they pumped more and more chemicals into me to try and counteract the poison that had seeped into my blood and my organs and my nervous system. They told me that I was lucky; my organs were close to failing, I should thank God that I was alive. It was as if they were rubbing it in my face. I didn't want them to save my organs.

On the third day, they pronounced me fully alive. They unstuck the tacky stickers on my chest and ankles and stomach, and rushed saline solution through my cannula so I felt icy cold rippling up through my veins. They did one more blood test and left the cannula in. Just in case.

They sent a psychiatrist and a support worker to see me in the outpatient ward: Dr. Chance and Jacob. Dr. Chance was wearing a feminist pantsuit. Jacob had a mildly uncomfortable expression on his face, but I couldn't place an emotion. Dr. Chance took out a packet of gum from her bag and looked at me. I twisted my hand around a rubber band I'd found in the corridor, watching the tips of my fingers turn slowly red. There was a Mickey Mouse Band-Aid on my knuckle from where my cannula had been removed and I focused on the dark bruising from where the nurse had gotten the blood test wrong twice. I think my parents were in the building somewhere, but I didn't want to see them. I couldn't face what I'd done to them, not yet.

"Would you like a piece?" Dr. Chance held out a strip of gum in the space between us. I shook my head. She took it for herself and began to chew slowly and methodically. "Have you eaten anything?"

"No," I said. "I still feel sick." I tensed my fist and watched as the veins seemed to rush to the surface of my skin.

"I'm not surprised—that antidote is nasty stuff—but you really should; your body's been through a lot in the last few days. Shall I ask the nurses to get you a sandwich?"

I didn't respond. I just looked at her as pointedly as she was looking at me, until she lowered her gaze. We sat in silence.

"God, it's hot in here," Jacob said, peeling off his jumper. "That's the thing with hospitals, they just can't seem to regulate their temperature . . ."

"Can we open a window?"

Both Jacob and Dr. Chance stood up and fumbled with the latch on the sticky window.

"That's better," Dr. Chance said, shooting me an awkwardly warm smile. "Now, where do you want to start? How are you doing at the moment?"

I shrugged.

"Scale of one to ten?" Jacob interjected unhelpfully.

"Two, maybe three, I guess."

"So, not fantastic," said Dr. Chance with an air of forced sympathy. "You've had quite the few days, so I'm not surprised." She paused and scribbled something on her pad of paper. I didn't wonder what she was writing. I just flicked the rubber band against my skin and focused on the sting-ing it brought with it.

"And tell me, how has your sleep been recently?"

Recently? Hours? Weeks? Months?

"Fine. I mean, I sleep."

"How many hours on average? Eight? Nine?"

"Something like that."

Jacob's phone went off. He stared at the screen for a few seconds, then switched it to silent.

"Sorry about that," he said. Dr. Chance gave him the same falsely jovial beam she had given me.

"How about eating?" she said. "I know you're not hungry now, but how has your appetite been in general?"

I didn't reply. What was the point? Ticktock.

"OK," she said softly, scribbling something on her notepad. "Can we talk about what happened, would that be all right?"

She was going to ask me about it even if it wasn't all right.

"Take your time," said Jacob unhelpfully. "We're not in a hurry."

I told them what happened. I told them what I did, how I did it, how tight the noose felt as it dug into my soft flesh, how my eyeballs felt like they were going to burst out of my sockets and I could feel my brain swelling against my skull, and how all at once the rail had broken, and I had fallen onto my bedroom floor with a crash, and how I had the bruises on my knees to prove it.

"Did you want to die? Was that your plan?"

Oh, OK, you asked it. You've said it now.

"There wasn't a plan," I responded, my gaze returning to the rubber band on my wrist.

"I understand. But what were you thinking at the time? What were you thinking when you overdosed?"

"I wanted . . . I don't know, I wasn't thinking much . . ." I said. "It's difficult to say."

"We know it's difficult to say, Tamar, but we need you to really try so that we can work out how best to help you," said Jacob, patronizingly. "We're not mind readers." They both laughed.

"I don't need your help," I snapped.

"Why not? Do you think you don't deserve it?"

I needed to get out. They were staring at me, the leg-pulling, gum-chewing pair of them, demanding an answer that I could not give so that they could tap into the computer: *We asked her. We assessed her risk and she told us she wasn't suicidal. Sorry, but it's not our fault she's now dead. It's not our fault she lied.*

"The reason why we ask this is because we're worried about you. We're wondering if an admission to an inpatient unit might help keep you safe. It's not far, and it wouldn't be for long . . ."

And before I knew it, I was standing up and I was swearing and shouting and storming out of the room. I was angry. How could they *say* that? Did they not understand? And they had laughed, as if it was funny. It wasn't funny at all.

"Piss off, you fucking, *fucking* idiots!"

And then there were other people around the nurses' station and I had to get away, so I turned around and ran into the toilet. I could hear someone calling my name behind me but I didn't care. The lock was stiff but I pulled it across and I remember vaguely hoping that it would never open again. The ceiling seemed an awfully long way away and I squeezed the side of the toilet with one hand and clenched my hair in a fist with the other. It was just me and four walls, four shiny white walls with chipped paint. There was noise from the outside of the room, I could hear it, but it was muffled and for a few seconds I made absolutely no noise just in case someone heard me breathe. And then the four walls spun and blurred and I couldn't hold back the tears anymore. And they came fast and tumbled down my face and I knelt on all fours and watched them fall onto the floor. Drip, drip.

"Oh, shit. Shit, shit, *shit*." This could not be happening. And I collapsed back onto the floor and felt my whole body heating up. Banged my head against the wall softly and the rhythm of it offered some comfort. There was only one voice outside the door now. I could barely register what he was saying but his voice held steady and calm and somehow it leached into my frantic mind. I groaned and rolled over onto my side like my stomach hurt, which perhaps it did. At that moment, everything hurt.

"Tamar, why don't you open the door and we can talk?" He carried on speaking but his voice was lost in another wave of uncontrollable despair and I crouched, face against the floor, not caring about hygiene, not caring that I could smell the musty material and make out every imperfection in it, not caring that the tears were streaking down my face and soaking into my pajamas.

I can't do this. I can't. Oh, God. Please make it end. Then I grabbed my neck with my two hands and squeezed it tightly, digging my nails into the sweaty skin, and looked up. The ceiling was so far away but suddenly the walls felt like they were closing in and I couldn't even stretch my legs out fully. This was how it was going to end. I'd be swallowed by a tiny room with no daylight, gasping for air, crying and crying, vision fuzzy. And I let go of my neck and watched color flowing back into my white fingertips and took a large gulp of air.

"Tamar, if you don't come out, I'm going to call the police." Did he say that? I don't know. Perhaps I needed an excuse to leave that room before it swallowed me whole, but I forced my way to my knees and slid back the lock and used the doorknob to pull myself up and opened the door. I stared into the face of someone who was quite insane, with hair that was matted and static and dyed an uncomfortable shade of pink. Her face was too white in some places and too red in others; snot had somehow made its way to above her eyebrows. In the few moments it took to notice that this was *me*—I had become this—Jacob had gone into the toilet and was thrusting more tissues than necessary into my trembling hands. I blew my nose. Soaked the paper in water and used it to wipe my face, like that was the problem.

Jacob took me into the corridor and filled up a cup of water from the machine. I bit my lip, trying to stop the relentless flow of tears.

"Shall we go back into the room?" said Jacob. I nodded

numbly and followed him. "You can have the sofa." I ignored him and sat in the chair closest to the door and buried my head in my hands and started bawling again. *Why can't I control myself?* My anger had dissipated slightly but now all that was left was a dull hollowness in my chest, which fell somewhere between fear and confusion. I could feel my whole body shaking. I was grateful for my hair because, although it was dry and tangled, it offered a curtain between me and the room around me.

Whenever I consider cutting my hair short I remember the way it protected me from the world for those few minutes and I change my mind.

I'd heard about psychiatric hospitals. I knew that they restrained you and forced injections into you and threw you into padded cells if you didn't behave. I wasn't mad. How could they do that?

I attempted to make myself look more presentable,

changed into clothes. I turned on the taps and held my hands under the cold until they began to ache, then swapped them to the hot tap and splashed my face, dried it with the paper from the dispenser. My arm itched under the dressings.

We walked slowly through the parking lot. I calculated my every move: how I was walking, how I held my arms, how fast I breathed. I was horribly aware of myself. Jacob started to tell me a story about some ducks but he had lost me by the second sentence and I tuned out. I wanted to get away and disappear into the alleys and curl up and die without anyone disturbing me or trying to convince me that life was worth living. Then, all of a sudden, I found myself running in the opposite direction, but I didn't get far because my legs buckled, like I was made of rotten wood, and I sat down on the parched pavement, my head spinning. Jacob stooped down to my level, a slight smirk on his face.

"What was that about?"

"I–I can't be fucked . . ." And I tried to smile back at him but I felt tears creeping back into my eyes so I bit my lip and stood back up. "I'm not going to run away."

"Listen, we've found you a bed. It's a little farther away than we'd hoped, but you can go tonight."

Collect your thoughts and travel two towns to the west.

"It's for your own safety, we're just trying to keep you safe. It won't be for long. Lime Grove is a nice place. It's not as scary as it sounds, don't worry about it, you'll be looked after there. I'm afraid I can't allow you to go home to pack, Tamar; your parents will do that tomorrow. You need to head to Lime Grove as soon as possible. I can give you a lift if you really can't go with your parents. If you're quick, you might even be there in time for dinner!"

We didn't speak on the journey. Jacob turned Radio 1 on and laughed at the unfunny jokes the presenters made. We got caught at every red light there was and I sat there and thought about how this showed that the whole world was against me; I was hated, even by traffic lights. I didn't blame the world. I was a murderer, after all. Jacob took a route

I wasn't used to—a stretch of motorway, through three roundabouts, past a McDonald's, down winding roads creeping through dreary suburbs, and over one toll bridge.

Turn off down a badly maintained road past the hospital and buzz the gates at the end, get greeted by the drone of a bored-sounding receptionist in front of a computer. Wait for the gates to creak open with a shudder.

It was a low-set, poorly painted white building with slabs of gray concrete still exposed near the bottom. There was a small, token lime tree near the front door.

Jacob knew the nurses and they greeted one another with shouts and aggressive handshakes. The receptionists were protected by a screen in case someone tried to kill them. They made sure that the front door was shut and bolted in two places before they opened the door that led out of the waiting room.

I walked through it to the other side.

 NoW

The park is saturated in mud from the April shower earlier in the day; it has spread from the grass onto the gravel paths that entwine their way through the trees. The playground to my right looks older than when I last came here a few years ago; the swings are rustier and they creak in the breeze, and the seesaw has lost the bright scarlet color it once had. A small child and his father sit morosely in the soggy sandpit, half-heartedly scooping the heavy sand into buckets.

"OK, then," says Dad, sitting down on the nearest bench, Brew panting by his side, like he can't imagine anything worse than a jog.

"Dad," I start. I'm not sure what I'm going to say.

"Sorry," he says stiffly. "I'm sorry."

"Why?" I reply, though I know why.

"It's just . . . It's nice to be spending time with you again. It's nice that you're getting better. Off you go . . ."

It's like I am the dog: He has released me to dart into the bushes, chase squirrels up trees, bark at my own shadow as it flickers between the leaves. Freedom—for a limited time only.

I don't know if I should stretch like I used to before I started to run. I try to touch my toes but find I can't reach. Good start.

My feet feel stiffer than they used to as I speed up into a jog, shoes slapping against the wet ground and spewing mud onto the backs of my calves. I follow the path around to where I used to go: steeply up, dodging smooth tree roots that swell out of the ground, and brambles that snatch like gnarled claws at my ankles as I go. My heart flutters. I'm not used to it doing this. I remember strong, consistent heartbeats that pounded with every step forward that I took, not confused taps like a bad drummer. I turn around and see my dad staring down at his phone on the bench below me. I can just disappear and he won't know. I shake my head to eject the thought and carry on running, even though my legs have started to ache and a stitch is gnawing in my side. This isn't like me. I don't get stitches. Or, at least, I didn't two years ago. The path curves around and the lake lies in front of me, dark and still. A swan courses through the middle, and it would be romantic if it wasn't for the extent of the algae squatting along the banks, collecting the rubbish that has been thrown in—parking tickets, empty bags of chips, a Sainsbury's shopping cart perched above the water.

One, two, one, two. The mud splats have reached my thigh. That is OK. Mud is OK. My heart rate begins to level out. A duck quacks indignantly and runs across the path in front of me, its feathers ruffled, as if I've disturbed its sleep in the reeds. I'm running . . . In my head there are other runners beside me, and I feed off their energy, their eyes fixed low on the ground, their necks sticky with sweat, their breathing . . . I can run faster, faster than every person I overtake and faster with every person I overtake, my legs slicing through the air faster than I want to go.

The fog that wandered into my brain and made its home there years ago, snuggled around my prefrontal cortex, lifts. It doesn't go away, but it lifts. If Dr. Flores wants to know what number I'm on now, I'd give him a nine. I am alive.

My daydream ends when I'm suddenly aware of my phone vibrating in the tight pocket of my Lycra leggings, buzzing against my thigh. The fog flops back down. People don't call me. Panting for breath (it could be the running; it could be the panic), I pull it out.

It's Toby.

I don't like phone calls. I don't like the fact that you can't see the person on the other end of the line. You don't know if they're laughing at you or laughing with you, or cursing you into the flaming pits of hell. You can't see their expression or their body language. You can't guess what they're thinking.

Trembling, I press "Accept" and hold the phone to my ear.

"Hi," I say.

"Hi," says Toby.

"Hi," I repeat.

"Yeah, hi, sorry, I was just ringing because your dad told me you had your phone today. I wanted to see how things were."

"They're good," I say.

"Look, I'm sorry about my party."

"That's all right," I say. "I don't really remember it much anyway. I'm sorry, too, though. I probably ruined it for everyone."

He laughs. Is he disappointed?

"You don't remember?"

"Nah," I say. "Not a thing."

"Oh, OK, then. Cool . . . I'll let you get on with it."

What would Elle do? Fuck it.

"Wait. I—shall we hang out some time? Next weekend?"

"Yeah, sure. Count me in." I think he's smiling.

There has been a shift in Elle over the past week. Everyone has felt it. She's crossed some invisible canyon on a tightrope and found that the grass is not greener on that side.

It starts when Alice is discharged. She leaves with her mum's arm tight around her back, her dad clutching her suitcase, and her brother tugging at her coat. Elle hugs her and steps back with a curious expression on her face. I can't tell exactly what she is thinking, but I understand it. It isn't fair.

Something has changed. It isn't obvious what, but her nursing observations increase to one check every five minutes. A torch flashing every five minutes in the night. Her slots from the shower schedule have remained unused for the past five days; ten minutes extra of wasting time running water over cold hands in the bathroom for the rest of us.

She still talks and eats with us at mealtimes and goes to school; she hasn't fallen into a cavernous pit of depression where staring at the wall is the only thing to do, but something is different. I think we noticed the change before she did—quietly spoken comments about "Does anyone have a right to live?" and sweating that makes her palms so clammy that the cutlery slips in her fingers and clatters to the floor. The nurses take her blood pressure every morning and every evening to check that the nervousness in her brain isn't about to cause a heart attack. Before, she wanted to talk about traveling to distant countries and starting psychiatric hospital revolutions, but now Dr. Flores prescribes her double the dose of lamotrigine and makes sure that a nurse watches her take it with two cups of water, and she speaks about death more than she does life.

The shift is even more pronounced when Dr. Flores doesn't write her up the leave she's hoped for on the weekend—she still has nowhere to go—and her usually mild manner turns and she lashes out like an angry cat, outstretched claws and tear-filled eyes. I hug her as she cries into my shoulder, her face so flushed you can't even see her freckles, desperate for the familiarity of being jolted from foster parents to respite carers to foster parents that the outside world holds.

At her tribunal, the doctors make it clear that Elle will not be meeting the outside world anytime soon, especially not with the way things are going at the moment. She remains sectioned under the Mental Health Act so that they can continue to pump her up with the medication that isn't helping her—it's too late—and deny her the freedom and the ability to live as more than just another statistic. Because she "can't make decisions for herself"; her brain is just too far gone, they say. I think that is how she sees it, anyway. It crushes her.

I am already awake by the time a piercing whistle screeches into my bedroom. I sit bolt upright in alarm; there must be an emergency. It sounds different, though—it has a friendlier tone, somehow, not the screech marking imminent panic I'm used to. Nurse Will sweeps open my bedroom door, swinging the whistle around his forearm.

"I've adopted a new technique to wake you lot up," he says with a grin, putting the whistle to his lips again. It sounds more feeble now that I know it isn't an emergency.

"You're so weird," I mutter, turning over in bed and trying to convince myself it isn't morning.

"You're the one in the psychiatric ward," he says. Not many people can get away with saying that, but Nurse Will can. I laugh.

"Don't be so rude," I say.

He blows the whistle again in response and swaggers out of the room, looking pleased with himself.

It takes twenty minutes after getting up and dressing in the first clean clothes I've worn in a week to realize that Elle isn't here. The door to her bedroom is ajar and the curtains haven't been opened, but she isn't in there.

Jasper comes down for breakfast this morning still dressed in his purple pajamas, disdain radiating from his face as he nibbles Corn Flakes into minuscule pieces, but the space where Elle should be sitting next to me is empty. I don't say anything. Patient Will notices that she isn't there, too. He doesn't say anything, either, but I see him staring at the empty plastic chair as he scrapes jam out of the plastic packaging. A nurse looks at us, as if daring us to question Elle's disappearance.

"I don't like blackberry jam," Patient Will says instead.

"There's some strawberry in the box," says the nurse.

"I've finished now," he replies quietly.

"Maybe tomorrow, then, Will."

Sit-down and morning meeting and morning snack and an hour of school pass laboriously and in an apathetic trance, waiting for Elle to walk in shouting, "Surprise!" Lime Grove doesn't feel right without Elle. It feels like an infinitely unhappier place.

Finally, at lunchtime, I can't wait any longer. She hasn't turned up and no one has uttered a word about her all day, and I'm beginning to wonder whether her existence has been a figment of my imagination.

"Where's Elle?" I ask, putting a greasy chip in my mouth and turning to Patient Will.

"Ran off, apparently. Ask Jasper, he seems to know more than anyone," says Patient Will as he twirls the gray haddock around his fork with undisguised disgust.

"She's run away? Again?"

Will nods. "This morning. She's been gone for hours. Didn't you notice?" He turns his attention to the wrinkled pile of peas instead, scooping them up and shoveling them into his mouth.

I have noticed. Of course I've noticed. Jasper prods the bowl of Jell-O in front of him with a teaspoon.

"It's not as bad as it looks," says the nurse at Ruby table. "You don't even have to chew it." She makes a point of scraping her own bowl, because the Jell-O is obviously so damn delicious that she can't bear to leave a single bit.

"Oh," I say. I can't think of a response.

"They've called the police already," says Jasper when I ask him during his post-lunch sit-down. "I heard them on the phone. They said she's a 'high-risk missing person.'"

This escape isn't like the Great Escape, and we both know it. It isn't going to be happy happy dancing dancing; Elle has slammed so hard down to rock bottom in the past week that the energy she expended spinning in circles and skipping during our escape is going to turn into agitation and pain and it is not going to end well. I say rock bottom. Rock bottom is actually a really difficult thing to define. There are times when you think you've crashed to the rock at the bottom, only to discover that you were actually hanging by your fingertips from the ledge just above it. Rock bottom is always far lower and far darker than you think.

"How did she get out again?" Why weren't they watching her? Why did they let her get away?

"Don't have a clue." Jasper sighs. "She's been gone since before breakfast, though, so it must've been when the night shift was still on. Maybe they were tired."

"Yeah, because that's a fantastic excuse," I say, waiting for him to smile. He's too worried about Elle to smile. So am I; she could be anywhere, doing anything at all. She could be dead.

We file solemnly into the classroom. No one complains about going to school for an extra two hours today, not even Harper. She sits down and draws a spider diagram with a red whiteboard pen and hardly moves for the next hour, except to pick up the paper she's using and wipe the table with her sleeve where the pen has run through.

A trainee teacher tries to explain the Cuban Missile Crisis with a globe and some Post-it notes, but I don't care about the Bay of Pigs invasion; I care about whether Elle is alive or dead or just existing, so not a single date is branded into my memory. Or perhaps he's just a terrible teacher. He pulls a tissue from his sleeve and wipes sweat from his forehead.

"So, from this, what can we say with regards to how the development of nuclear weapons has affected our attitudes to warfare?"

No one wants another mushroom cloud engulfing innocent people. That's obvious. What's the question, again?

The trainee teacher leaves me with a pen and two thin sheets of unlined paper so I can use my broken brain to create five hundred perfect words on what happened in Cuba in 1962. I spin the globe around twice until I find Cuba, covered by a tangerine Post-it note that hides half of Mexico from view as well.

Flip a coin. Is she dead or is she alive?

I tie my greasy hair back into a ponytail, then undo it and braid it instead and try to convince myself that I'm doing everything I can to stop the terrible seconds from passing. Harper rips out another piece of paper from the pad next to her, swaps to a green marker-pen, and continues with her spider diagrams. From the other side of the room, Jasper listens to Maureen drone on about symbolism in *The Picture of Dorian Gray*. I'm not sure if he is actually listening, but he nods methodically in all the right places and sweeps a highlighter over the pages of the book every so often.

"It's very much a work of philosophy, a novel that's really supposed to make us think . . ."

"Yeah, yeah . . ."

"So, what can we say about the portrait? Is it supposed to just be a picture of Dorian Gray, or does it represent something more?"

"It represents something more," repeats Jasper in a bored tone.

"Quite," says Maureen, adjusting her false teeth.

The police turn up at Lime Grove just as the lessons end, at three o'clock, and they stomp in with their heavy black boots and upturn everything in Elle's room: the mattress on her bed, every single sock. I don't know what they're looking for. We are kept in the dining room as their search starts to extend to the rest of the building—in case she's left a cryptic note crumpled behind the DVD rack in the lounge or in among the towels in the linen cupboard. They probably find a lot of things: the gunky wax strips that Alice tried to use before discovering they were too sticky and out of date, the broken cigarette lighter that had somehow sneaked its way into the magazine box last week, underneath the thin pages of *Take a Break*. They don't find any clues to Elle's whereabouts. In fact, there's no sign of any developments regarding Elle at all until late into the evening, after dinner, when Harper starts and points out of the lounge window.

Elle is being supported out of the ambulance by a paramedic and a policeman. She can walk, but she holds tightly onto their wrists, and they do the same to her, arms interlocked. She isn't wearing any shoes or socks, her pale feet tentative on the tarmac as she heads toward the front door. On one side of her forehead is a dressing, blood seeping through. Her hair has been tied back by someone. She didn't do that. Elle never wears her hair back.

Two chimes of the bell.

I don't see her for an hour, even though I know she is in the building. The viewing slat to Therapy Room 1 is closed and

I can't even hear muffled voices from the other side like usual; they must be whispering.

I catch a snippet of conversation with her when she comes out. Someone has taken her dressing off. She has three stitches embedded in her forehead.

"Where did you go?" I say, pulling her into a hug. She smells of petrol and earth.

"He found me," she whispers. "It was so far from everywhere, but he found me just as the train was coming."

"What? Elle!" I'm not sure what she's saying but I want to cry. "Who found you?"

"I don't know, I don't know. I think he was a workman or something. He pushed me so hard that I just collapsed onto my head in a clump of nettles. I'm so sorry."

"I'm glad you're OK," I say.

The stitches on her forehead wrinkle as she forces a smile.

"Elle," says Nurse Will, coming out of Therapy Room 1. "Let's go and get your head dressed again, please."

She meekly follows him upstairs and into the clinic room.

No one wants to talk for the rest of the evening; even the TV hasn't been turned on to detract from the uncomfortable silence. The whole ward, in fact, remains entirely quiet for hours—until, that is, the middle of the night.

It starts with a few thumps from the bedroom next to me, moans and the sound of something being dragged across the carpet, before picking up into hollering and groaning in the corridor and beyond, into the lounge.

I hear Elle's maddened cries for the next half an hour, as she thumps on the corridor walls outside the bedroom, dashing and darting away from nurses who want to inject her, and screaming wildly. I don't look out the window or my door, but I'm sure if I did, I would see the chairs that I heard land, flying across the corridor and slamming into the walls, magazines hurled and ripped up on the floor.

"Get away from me, get away!" she moans, as if they've rounded upon her wielding axes and bows and arrows.

I slam my pillow over my head to block out her guttural cries, hoping that a nurse doesn't come in and think I am trying to smother the air out of my lungs.

"Stop it, stop it, stop it!"

The lights in the corridor aren't turned out at eleven thirty like they usually are. Elle is far too awake and far too frightened to recognize the quiet that the night should bring.

She must keep out of their reach for quite some time, sprinting wildly around the ward in a bewildered frenzy, but they catch her finally, because by two in the morning I finally drift into unconsciousness; the ward has gone quiet, but for the soft beeping of the smoke alarm above my head. The muffled voices of a few nurses penetrate the walls of my bedroom, but I can't hear what they are saying. Jangling keys lock the bathroom doors because of weigh-in in a few short hours. They don't want any patients filling themselves to the brim with "not drinking" water before they step tentatively onto the scales at 6 a.m. The night is silent. Finally, the corridor lights dim and I release my grip on the pillow over my head and allow myself to fall asleep.

Early in the morning, just as I wake up, Elle is being moved to a psychiatric intensive-care unit halfway across the country, in an ambulance with two nurses and a policeman. I see her climbing into it in the parking lot as I pull open my curtains too hard and they clatter to the floor. I run over to Emma in the lounge, but she says I can't see her; Elle is no longer a patient at Lime Grove. She needs space. I don't want to, but I start crying and I fall to the floor and crouch there, my too-short pajamas hitching up close to my knees.

The thought of Elle sitting in the back of a secure ambulance makes me want to be sick. I think of her freckled wrists locked together in handcuffs yesterday, and the bruises that must have formed there, the three small stitches in her forehead, the way she had sat, hunched, in reception, her small frame shrouded by the multitude of policemen blocking her vision.

Crying is different when it's not selfish. The pain comes from somewhere else entirely—the area around your heart, against your rib cage—in a relentless current of despair. Selfishness forms in the pit of the stomach. I want to pretend that Elle will be OK, but the truth is that I'm not sure she will be.

You could see emptiness in her eyes, her vacant, faraway expression that she had all of yesterday evening. I don't think she wanted to do things differently. I wonder if she was thinking anything at all as the ambulance slowly headed up the rush-hour motorway toward a hospital beyond Birmingham. I can't imagine that anything is happening in her mind. Her mind has defeated her.

I didn't help her. I didn't help her, like I didn't help Iris. Maybe "couldn't" is a better word.

Nurse Will offers me a marshmallow from the pack the night staff have left, because he can't find any tissues but he wants to do something, I suppose. I take it, but it doesn't melt in my mouth; my gums and my tongue are too dry, so I have to chew it like rubber. Elle is magnificent and vibrant and I feel like I'm mourning someone with all my heart even though she is not dead.

"She'll be all right. They're good, where she's going. They'll help her."

"Will she even remember me?" Will I be anyone to her? Yesterday, her face had been so distant, I wondered if she recognized me at all.

"Of course she'll remember you, Tamar. You only lived together. Go and get some clothes on, now, it's nearly time for breakfast."

Life. People roll along in a money-grabbing, stiff-upper-lipped blur. Like a shoal of fish moving with the tide toward the ultimate prize of death.

Elle wasn't one of those people. She never wanted to follow the mindless clump of tired people; she wanted excitement and laughter and dances at midnight in shimmering gardens. She wanted to live hungrily and feast on slices of life that other people didn't find, make noise and change human nature. That's how I thought of her, at least.

At first, I hope for a letter, a text, a token from her to let me know that she is OK, but it doesn't come. Her Facebook account is deactivated weeks later and I hope that means she is alive. I want her to be alive. But I don't know.

I think Dr. Flores has developed a lot more wrinkles since he met me. Sitting in his swivel chair in front of his desk, I can't help but notice that his face is lacking the false smoothness that radiated from it when I first met him. The bookshelf has been removed from his office, which is probably my fault as well. The Holy Bible that cracked the screen of his computer sits underneath his arm on the desk—just in case I disrespect it in such a spectacular fashion again. He isn't wearing his periodic table tie, or any other tie, today.

Perhaps he remembers how much they offended me. Doesn't want to get on my wrong side again.

I haven't realized that he's religious until now, and somehow it doesn't suit him. I imagined him as such a stickler for the "evidence-based" and "logical reasoning" side of life. Strange.

He waits for me to start talking. I read the cards from ex-patients on his corkboard. Apparently, he saved Jodie's life, and Megan can't thank him enough. I guess these are things to be proud of. I open my mouth but don't say a thing. I want to talk about Elle and Iris and their red hair and their lives and how I couldn't save either of them, but Dr. Flores says it isn't my job to save anyone. I ask him if that's his job and, if so, why couldn't he save Elle? He says that it isn't his job.

I tell him that Jodie disagrees. He mutters about patient confidentiality and pushes the card shut.

"Do you fancy a discharge date?" he says suddenly, as if it's as easy as handing out sweets to children. My lips must move into some kind of negative because before I have a chance to answer he says: "What's wrong? You know this is a good thing?"

"Is it?" I think out loud (which I suppose is what talking really is, anyway). "Yeah, I suppose it is."

When Alice found out her discharge date she had pranced around the sitting room with glee in her eyes, and wrote the date in bubble writing on the whiteboards in the lounge and the dining room, and the blackboard in the art room so that no one could forget. Dr. Flores is probably looking for my spark, too.

"You haven't attempted suicide for some time," he says. I try to stop my mind from turning his words into an insult.

The worse things get, the higher people's thresholds become for what constitutes "OK." When I first started scratching myself every so often, ever so little, everyone was stunned into shock and it was all, QUICK, *grab the scissors, this is awful, she must stop stop stop.* Then, when the self-harm got worse, one doctor suggested that I go back to using scissors because then at least there wouldn't be a terrible risk of damaging tendons and paralyzing my arm, because I couldn't possibly continue the way I was, self-harming like that all the time.

Now the threshold has been raised even higher, by the looks of things. *Self-harm all you want, by all means chop off your arm for all we care. You're not dead, so you must be doing great. Here, have a pat on the back. Have a discharge date.*

"What do you think happened to Iris?" he asks suddenly.

"I killed her." It's a relief to say it.

I thought Dr. Flores would stare at me, his eyes goggling and horrified. He doesn't. He just puts his pen down on the desk beside him and turns his chair ninety degrees, his expression that of blissful unconcern. I'm unnerved, and I get the impression he is waiting for me to expand, but I have nothing more to say. A balloon has burst inside me.

"You killed her? Can you tell me how you did that?" He isn't making notes anymore; he's just watching me through his scratched glasses.

"It was—I—it was an accident. We were drunk, she was more drunk . . ."

The digital clock beeps ten o'clock.

"Tamar," Dr. Flores says. "Iris committed suicide. She killed herself—the coroner's report said so. Surely you know that?"

THEN

Iris was shy when we first met. Her family moved around a lot, so much that everyone assumed they were on the run. She'd been to three schools in one year. She didn't speak much at first, just busied herself at the back of the room, scratching intricate doodles in red fountain pen in the corners of textbooks. She wore her hair in two French braids smoothed tightly around her ears.

Iris was good at art, and you could see it in her expression as she drew. Mia and I used to watch her from the other end of the art table, scratching PVA from our fingers. Mia didn't like the way the art teachers swooned over Iris like they'd found the next Picasso. She told me she was going to ruin Iris's drawing before she did it.

Paint splattered. Mia gasped, fixed her eyes on Iris. "Oh my gosh!" she said, reaching for the nearest cloth and scrubbing at the drawing so that the dark strokes on the paper smudged even more. "I am so sorry . . ."

Iris's blackened hands quivered. "Don't worry," she whispered. "It's OK."

"You can fix it," I said, when Mia had gone. "Think of Tracey Emin. She just unmade a bed."

Iris smiled, properly this time. "I guess. Thanks."

"In twenty years' time, people will say that the paint on your drawing represents the decay of humanity or something. Just touch up the lines around the hairline."

Iris obliged quietly and obediently.

After that, she followed me like a magnet. She started smoking just so she could stand outside the school gates with us. She started talking more, too. She actually had a lot to say, but that didn't save her life.

One morning, when it was so cold you didn't have to have a cigarette to breathe smoke, when there was no one else to see, Mia lifted the lighter to Iris's red hair.

Iris's face said it all before the flames did, and her hair billowed into a smoking russet plumage. Someone who wasn't me engulfed Iris's head in a blazer, the school crest beaming gold and gray through the flames.

By the time the ambulance arrived, Iris wasn't on fire. She was just sitting by the school gates with teeth chattering louder than an angry squirrel and sheens of crimson lining her scalp. Shiny tracks of peeled skin running across her forehead. The paramedics gave advice about dressings and cleaning wounds, then left her to it, because the burns weren't that bad. She disappeared into school without another glance in my direction, and I didn't follow her. Not immediately, at least.

"She didn't find it funny," I muttered quietly in Mia's direction, eventually.

"What?" said Mia sharply.

The teachers frog-marched us back to their offices. They knew we smoked every day, and they knew it was illegal, and now they were wishing they hadn't turned such a blind eye.

"What happened?"

"It was an accident," Mia said. "Tamar didn't mean to . . . She was lighting her cigarette and she didn't look properly . . . You know how long Iris's hair is . . ."

A grades make you untouchable, and she knew it.

Iris spent a lot of time disappearing from school after that. She was going to the dentist, to a tutor, to visit a llama farm . . . Mia left her alone, for the most part. We went to our detentions for a week and she got 100 percent on a math test and then the teachers forgot about it.

Sometimes I tried to speak to Iris, but she would shake her head and mutter quietly until I left.

She fooled me into thinking she was fine.

She left a suicide note in her underwear drawer in her bedroom, just above notes about cleaning out the fish tank and buying chocolate sauce for pancakes. It was short. I'm not sure what suicide notes are supposed to say; maybe there's a convention, but hers didn't say much.

Iris said that she was sorry, and she listed every person in her world who she knew would fall down and never quite get back up because of her death: her mum and dad, her cousin who spoke at her funeral. I wasn't on the list. I shouldn't have been affected by her death. She said, "I have died by suicide," the ebony words blasted out from the white background. That was it, as if she just wanted to make sure that everyone knew exactly why she had launched herself off the side of the dam, wearing her heaviest pair of boots, filled to the ankles with stones. She didn't want any room for confusion. She'd thought this through. It wasn't an accident.

The first thing that the police found on her phone was the text that I'd sent her: *Are you all right? xxx*

It had been sent at fourteen minutes past eleven, three

hours after Iris and I had last sat on the bank of the river, since we stood on the dam. She had been dead for three hours.

She'd left her phone on the rocks just where the dam met the wispy grass.

That day she'd joked about how life was crap and wouldn't it be better to just die than face another day of this shit.

I'd laughed and taken another swig of cider.

I'd laughed at Iris as she expressed the pain that she could not fight any longer in her ungraceful, drunken manner.

I'd left her next to the river as she planned her own death.

She reached out to me and I ignored her. No, I didn't ignore her; I *laughed*. And I told her to jump into the dam as a joke. That I would follow her. I lied.

Mia was right: I was the last person to see Iris alive and I didn't save her.

It was my fault she died.

NOW

You know I said that time in a mental hospital goes really, really slowly?

The last two weeks at Lime Grove fly past so quickly you'd be forgiven for thinking I'm having fun.

They hate you here, they hate you.

I spend three nights at home from Friday to Monday each weekend and I force myself out for a jog every morning, even though the risperidone makes my head spin. *Structure is the key. Practice the mindfulness that Janice taught you. Notice. Observe. Touch. Smell. Taste. Don't judge. Don't judge.*

The day that I'll become a free human being, away from locked doors and metal bolts and jangling jail keys, is looming closer and closer, and Jasper laughs at the horror on my face when anybody mentions it.

Sometimes someone comes up to me and says something like: "Tamar, well done. You're doing so well with your recovery."

Recovery is a funny concept, because in reality we're all recovering from something: a bad cold, a breakup, sex, drugs, rock and roll. No one gets to decide when you do it or how you do it, either. So when Emma or Nurse Will pats me on the back with "recovery" on their tongues—you're doing it right—I flinch a little.

Am. Not. Recovering.

Recovery means commitment and positivity.

And progress.

I am none of those things; the only thing that I am doing is trying, but we all know that's not good enough. You have to win, too.

They're getting rid of you because you're poisonous. They need a bed for someone who isn't evil, evil. These thoughts are worse when you're recovering.

I play a lot of Trivial Pursuit in those two weeks—more, I think, than I have during my whole admission. I learn most of the answers to the questions, too, like Patient Will did, so our games are faster than they were before, and I even win sometimes. The TV rule changes and they ban it until five in the evening, so we're forced to think about something other than the lie-detector results of who got whom pregnant.

I see Toby on both Saturdays, and before I see him I fret and fluster over what I'm going to wear, like a teenager who is so very normal, and it feels good. The is-my-dress-too-short panic brings me intense happiness, because this is what I am supposed to be worrying about, not why that person in the street is looking at me weirdly (either I've tucked my skirt into my underwear, or he's planning to stalk and rape me).

You aren't wanted at home. You aren't wanted at Lime Grove anymore. You aren't wanted anywhere, you bad, bad, bad person.

I pop back lorazepam like Smarties when the thoughts get too much, because that's what is in my care plan, and wait for it to zonk me out on the downstairs sofa (when bad thoughts happen, the rule is: Get to the communal parts of the house, quick, before you kill yourself). The nurses congratulate me on that: "Before, you wouldn't have done that, Tamar. You would have hurt yourself, wouldn't you?"

You're getting better at this whole life thing, Tamar.

I have twenty-eight meals and twenty snacks in these last weeks. Harper silently refuses to eat her share of twenty-eight meals and twenty snacks, so they shove her on bed rest and treat her pressure sores with a pressure mattress and give her food through a tube, so I see even less of her than before, apart from when they wheel her into the bathroom four times a day, and she sits there, back curled.

On the evening of my last night at Lime Grove, I burst into uncontrollable tears, and Jasper lends me his anti-stress coloring book and gel pens.

"Thanks," I say, between snuffles. "I'll use it tonight."

An agency nurse who doesn't know the rules lets me have a cigarette afterward, in the garden. The heat from the smoke dries my teary cheeks.

"Better?" she says, after I take a final puff and then pass the stub back to her to bin the evidence.

"Yeah," I say, despite the fact that it isn't better.

They hate you. Everyone hates you. Even you hate you. Get. Out.

"I need a zopiclone."

Emma disappears into the nursing room and watches me swallow the tablet without question. Even she understands that the risperidone won't quite hack it tonight.

I crawl into bed—the bed, my bed—and wait for the drugs in my body to bid me good-night. I sleep, eventually. Sleep is predictable. I don't dream.

It is so bittersweet, I'm not sure that I can stomach it. I unstick the photos of Brew with glasses on, of Toby and Elle, and Brew eating a pig's ear that have lived on the notice-board for long enough for dust to settle and muffle their shine. Nurse Will supervises my trash bag use (moving out = stress = trying to suffocate myself with strips of plastic) as I shove all my belongings into the bags without a second look.

"Do you really want those?" he says.

"What?"

He points at the wad of papers that I've stuffed, higgledy-piggledy, into the nearest bag.

"Yeah. I want them." My hands clutch my collection of case-management notes, which I requested. I press them against my stomach in an attempt to smooth out the creases.

Tamar is generally bright on ward. She continues to have

symptoms of persistent dysregulated mood and there is evidence of some cognitive rigidity in relation to DSH.

I put them on the bed. "I'll take them later."

Jasper hovers into view. He's wearing the same gray Batman T-shirt that he wore when we first met, only it isn't so baggy anymore. It doesn't sag from the pile of bones that used to make up his chest.

"Do you need any help?" he says. I nod.

Nurse Will doesn't say anything as Jasper comes into my room and kneels by the pile of clothes.

Tamar has gone AWOL from the ward on one occasion. The risk of her absconding again is medium.

"You've got a lot of stuff," he says, picking up a pair of leggings I didn't know I owned and folding them into my suitcase.

"It was a surprise to me, too."

He laughs.

"You made yourself too comfortable," he says with a grin vaguely in my direction.

"Obviously."

"This is not your home, it is a hospital," says Jasper in a nasal voice, imitating Emma with wagging fingers.

She continues to have delusional thoughts about killing a friend of hers two years ago, but does not experience any other psychotic symptoms. Her friend committed suicide. Tamar will need support in the community to deal with these irrational beliefs.

"You do not live here," Jasper finishes.

He is right; it isn't my home. My home doesn't have windows in the doors and anti-ligature curtains that collapse if you draw them too tightly. It doesn't have temperamental toilets with no seats or tattered carpets stained with God knows what, or frighteningly unwell people asleep in the room next door, or incredibly amazing people asleep in the room next door, breathing in time with the beeps from the smoke alarm on the ceiling. It doesn't have any of that.

Her symptoms are concurrent with that of a personality disorder (borderline).

Personality disorder?

"Don't cry," says Jasper, and Nurse Will materializes a

tissue from nowhere. They're good at doing that, nurses. Finding tissues. "These better be happy tears. You're free, you can do whatever you want!" Jasper's hand finds mine and I feel pressure squeezing against my fingers.

That is true. I can do absolutely anything I want in the whole wide world. I can bake a cake or read a book or run from Land's End to John O'Groats and then back again just for fun. I should ask Toby about that. We should do it. Why not?

I knew I was a bad person. I was right. I have a personality disorder.

I blow my nose too sharply, and my nose ring slips out, catching the tears as they tumble down.

"Yeah, they're happy," I splutter. I think they are, anyway.

"What d'you want me to do with this amazing creation?" says Jasper, holding up a papier-mâché elephant I made in art group a month ago.

"You can keep it."

"Very appropriate," he says, examining its tusks. "I am an elephant."

"You're not an elephant. You can't keep it if you say that," I say, making to grab it.

"No, no, I want it! I was joking," he says. Behind every joke there is a truth. I hate that he hates every inch of himself more and more as every week goes by and he gains a kilogram of fat. A kilogram of life, more like. "I'll call it Ellie."

"Very original, well done," I say between tears that make me gasp for air.

"Yeah, I thought so, too."

"Don't forget your things in the nurses' office," says Nurse Will. "I'll grab them."

He leaves me on the floor with the two trash bags that I could kill myself with. I hear his card swiping the office door open, my locker swinging open.

"You staying for lunch?" asks Jasper.

"I don't think so, no. My parents are supposed to be coming at eleven."

"But it's vegetable lasagna day!" he says indignantly. "You can't miss out on that."

I smirk. "Poor me." I'm not going to miss the cold plates of defrosted congealed slop disguised as food. Especially not the vegetable lasagna; the last time I ate it, my fork met ice crystals between layers of stodgy pasta and slippery peppers.

"OK," says Nurse Will brightly, kicking the door ajar with his foot and slamming a plastic box onto my bed. "In here, we have some incredibly dangerous items. Cue dramatic music . . ." He pulls it open and withdraws a pair of tweezers and a bottle of Bleach London Sea Punk hair dye with a flourish. "Use them wisely."

I haven't dyed my hair since I got here, and it's returned to the pale blonde color that I'd tried so hard to hide with layers of bubblegum pink and pastel blue. The girl by the river isn't my identity anymore.

"Oh, and this—" Nurse Will holds up a razor, its thin edges shining under the ceiling light, and hovers it in the air. "I think I might give that to your parents . . ."

I pull out the drawer of my desk. Glistening fragments of the DVD I'd once broken to cut myself with lie in shards around the incomplete worksheets that my school sent me months ago.

"Anyone for some source analysis?" I hold up a page of history notes.

"Going . . . going . . . gone," says Jasper, rapping his knuckles on the side of my bed as I cram the notes into the nearest trash bag.

My room looks different without the clutter littered all over the floor or the posters on the noticeboard above my bed. It's more clinical, somehow, like it isn't my room anymore. It is just Room Number 4 in the humorless bedroom wing of a psychiatric hospital, empty of any personality or warmth. Waiting for the next person to tiptoe in and set up home. I hope that they make it theirs in the same way that I've done. Not that it matters. I walk out into the corridor, holding back another wave of tears surging up my gullet, and peel off the name sign that Elle drew for me in her first week: swirls of gold and turquoise and smudged black ink. Now it can be anyone's door.

Five pieces of A4 paper have been stuck clumsily together

and taped to the wall of the lounge. It says "good-bye tamar" in sloppy lowercase writing and still-wet paint.

"Patient Will made it," Jasper says. "I saw him doing it in art group."

I feel a sudden and unexpected surge of affection. He hasn't come out to say good-bye, but the buzzing from his thoughts being transmitted and read by MI5 was screeching so loudly in his brain that he smashed his fist into the wardrobe so hard he broke two fingers and a thumb.

My parents arrive at eleven on the dot. Nurse Will unlocks the door to downstairs and I follow him, the trash bags clumping down each stair behind me.

"Bye, then," I say huskily as Jasper grabs my arms and pulls me into a hug tight enough to totally cut off the blood supply to everything below my waist. I know he doesn't like hugs—hugs mean that I can feel the bulges of fat swimming below the surface of his skin—so this hug means something. "Don't forget to eat up everything that's on your plate."

"Every scrap," he says with a grin, releasing his grip.

"Including breakfast."

"Of course," he says dismissively. "Breakfast's my favorite meal of the day!"

The reception area flashes before me. I need to remember every single detail—the photos of every member of staff that hang, lopsided, to the left of me, the rumbling water dispenser with its thin triangular cups, the threadbare cushions tossed lazily on the sides of broken plastic chairs. Slick patterned floors, obviously designed by someone who hates teenagers: nauseating flowers with beaming faces splattered across shades of gray. I want it to remain familiar, right down to the ruthlessly bleached smell, which is lost the farther you go into Lime Grove. The receptionist fiddles with her headset, then picks the gaps between her teeth with a single glittery false nail.

"Right, then, Tay, let's make a move," says Dad as he strides purposefully into the reception area, dragging my suitcase behind him. "No point in waiting for the grass to grow." He blinks and a piece of metal glints in his ear. An earring has been forced into the decade-old hole in his earlobe.

Actually, there's every point in waiting just a little bit longer. The moment that I step out onto the hard, dusty April ground, I'll be free. I can go home and dance and sing in the shower just because no one will see me, then eat a pint of Ben & Jerry's (there will be no one to watch me and scribble down "binging behavior" in my notes) in front of whatever "inappropriate" TV show that I want to watch. Fuck it, I could even watch *Come Dine with Me*. There will be no more tree worshipping in a dingy therapy room with Janice and her meaningful rings, or grazing my throat with undiluted doses of sedatives that I don't want.

Dr. Flores doesn't come to see me off, but it doesn't matter. He doesn't have to. Nurse Will unlocks the door to the outside world for the final time, with a disappointingly soft high five, and I step out of my cage like a tiger from a zoo.

THEN

The two girls had been drinking since three, a swig for every crash of the river. The Golden Virginia they were smoking like shriveled worms falling out of rolling paper. They tried to blow rings in the sticky air.

Failing.

Giggling.

Heads spinning. Could be the alcohol, could be the heat.

Now it was late, and the sky was pale pink, like the

smooth inside of a conch. Cans of cider glinted in the grass and trees flopped like vast ivory wigs, heavy from the weeks of rain. Henna patterned the girls' bare arms, a memory of windswept festivals bleeding color.

The first girl swigged.

The second girl made daisy chains the lengths of her legs. She picked them up and threw them into the river, where they floated like tiny lilies. A crow leered over a piece of over-grilled bacon discarded from a barbecue. It squawked, its black eyes shining. The girls talked.

The first girl beckoned to the surging river ahead of them, brown and black and foaming. They laughed. The second girl nodded.

Their fingers interlocked in a drunken clasp and they swayed as they stood up. The dam in front of them shouted.

"We're such idiots," said the blonde girl.

"Such idiots."

They stumbled over soapy tangles of moss and their calves turned pink at the cold. The branches of a dead tree sprawled like bones and the first girl's faded lilac streaks echoed the sunset.

"Jump, Iris," she said. "I'll follow you."

"It's cold, so fucking cold . . ."

"My dad's going to be here soon."

"You go first, then."

"Just jump . . ."

The engine of a car broke the silence, pulling up in the gravel of an invisible parking lot.

"My dad's here. I'd better go. See you at school?"

"Yeah." The second girl looked down at the dam.

"Do you want a lift?"

"No, don't worry, Tamar. I'll get the bus home."

The first girl shrugged OK, then turned and walked to the parking lot. She clicked open the door of the car and slumped onto the seat.

"Are you OK?" said her dad. "You look drunk."

"I'm fine." She turned the radio up louder and looked out of the window as her dad drove off, away from the drowning, away from Iris.

Iris put her boots back on and filled them with stones. She left her phone by the side of the river. She walked back onto the weir and jumped into the surging pool below. For a few seconds her body was tossed around as if all her bones had been removed. Then, as more cascades of white water tumbled over the weir, she disappeared, her hand lingering above the water for a few seconds, as if searching for something, anything. The roar of the river was all that could be heard. Clouds had crept into the sky and they were black and low and ready to burst.

NOW

"You ready?"

"I'm so out of practice," I say with a grimace.

"You're not! I heard you ran the warm-up in twelve minutes," says Toby with an air of envy. Twelve minutes to cover the stretch of a swampy field as it curls past sheep protected by one thin electric fence, and across the bridge at the end. Two opportunities for death in twelve minutes.

Being zapped into the stars.

Cracking onto the road six meters below.

"I wasn't the fastest," I say. "Loads of people beat me."

"Yeah, but they've been practicing."

I laugh at his earnest expression. "How do you know I haven't been practicing?"

"Whatever," he says with a grin. "May the best runner win?"

"May the worst runner lose," I reply, holding my hand out, but he pulls me against the slippery Lycra fabric he's wearing and holds me there a little longer than usual.

"You feel horrible," I say, stepping away from him. I don't think he's hurt, because he holds my hands in his and shakes them with so much exaggerated vigor I think my elbows are going to pop out of the sockets.

"So do you," he says smugly.

I peel off the waterproof jacket I'm wearing, static electricity fuzzing the ends of my arm hairs as a man in a megaphone calls us toward the start line, and throw it onto the pile of clothes someone has started next to a marshal in a yellow jumper. The secrets engraved into my arms are exposed to the world: the ghosts of thin white scars in methodical rows tracing every inch of my arm. The thick red scar along my left forearm, the faint marks of the stitches still peppered on each side like the railway tracks that Elle tried to hurl herself onto.

Enough. Focus on the run.

Focus on the gun.

The gun in the man's hand as he raises it into the air.

Bang.

I am supposed to be running. I need to run. The swarm of people thunders around me, megaphones booming with the voices of bored-sounding women. People jostle into me. I start to run. My eyes search for Toby and his too-tight Lycra, but everyone is dressed the same and I can't make him out in the blur of sinewy legs and fluorescent spiked shoes.

Do I want this?

My feet squelch into mud that every person in front of me has churned up, and each spike on my shoes sinks down, drifting into the earth. I'm settled in the middle of the pack as the gaps between runners grow, and I have space to move my arms and legs without worrying about barging into someone.

In through the nose, out through the mouth.

I focus my eyes on the gloopy ground in front of me; there's spitting rain and the smoky smell of sausages sizzling in fat in a food truck. The weather is the sort of unsettled, anemic white that precedes a rainbow. There might have already been a rainbow, but I'm too focused on the ground to see.

All I need to do is run: ignore the beady-eyed thoughts, like the crow by the river, clutching onto my neck, and move my feet. It is simple. Or at least, the theory is simple.

I don't win. I end up somewhere unspectacular, in the middle of the cluster, the sort of place where people would forget you. That's OK. I want to be forgotten. There are still hordes of stragglers bringing up the back as I stand at the food kiosk and squirt ketchup over the hot dog that I've been smelling for the past half an hour.

Toby comes and hugs me, and I feel the curved edges of his glinting silver medal digging into my chest bones. His arms, freckled with mud, brush against my own arms, bumpy and pale and exposed to the world.

"You did it!" he says, delighted. "You did amazing."

"I did fairly average. You did amazing," I retort.

"You didn't. You were good."

"Thanks," I say.

"So . . . chips?"

"I just got this!" I say, holding the hot dog up toward his nose.

"No, I mean, we should go get them from town. You know, for old times' sake."

"All right," I say. "Let me just tell my parents, though. If they notice I've disappeared, I'll be on the police's missing-persons radar within a minute."

"Really?" He grimaces.

"You clearly don't know my parents," I say, laughing.

We take Toby's car into town—his battered old burgundy Volkswagen Golf that his aunt loaned him when he passed his test.

"Just shove everything onto the floor," he says, indicating the lighters and dirty running socks and open first-aid boxes that gild the leather seats.

I can't help but wonder how he managed to pass his test; he stalls on roundabouts and sends a foul burning smell through the car as he shudders up a hill in completely the wrong gear. He laughs so hard that he ends up slamming his forehead into the top of the steering wheel when he accidentally accelerates through a red light. If I hadn't been fearing for my life, I probably would have laughed with him. Look at that—I'm fearing for my life. I must be enjoying myself; congratulations to Toby, the boy who's made me fear for my life.

"Slow down, Toby, for God's sake!" I yell as he swerves

violently around a ninety-degree corner, hacking up the groaning gear stick into position.

"I am," he replies. "Don't interfere with my driving!"

"Don't drive like a lunatic, then," I reply, and he tuts, and before I know it the car has stopped and he's sprawled across the steering wheel shaking with laughter, and I'm laughing at him because his hair has fallen over it like a stream of falling leaves and he's shaking like a leaf and he's covered in mud like autumn leaves.

We both laugh because we know that I am the lunatic.

He pulls himself together and starts to drive again.

I turn up the radio and listen to the pounding of Eminem so I won't notice the speed.

It's all about distractions. It works.

I don't unpack for quite a few weeks after I arrive home. I don't want to. The trash bags and my suitcase sit expectantly in the corner of my bedroom day after day, waiting for me to empty them and spread the posters over my blank walls where they used to be, to cover the ghosts of Blu Tack still clinging to the walls. It takes some time for it to feel like home again. The curtain rail that I pulled from its socket and cracked in two is gone, so I have to tuck towels over the top of my window to block out the pale early-morning light that April has brought with it. Brew, as well, takes some time before he clambers onto my bed again and sleeps at the foot of it, his hefty presence heating my feet and my ankles like he used to, his left canine exposed as he snores gently and rhythmically in his sleep. I stick the name sign that Elle made for me on my bedroom door as soon as I arrive, though. I unpack that. At least I can pretend that I'm in Lime Grove, with its four low walls and locked doors.

I don't miss it, exactly. Psychiatric hospitals aren't the sort of places that you miss, but I do wonder what's happening there, and how long it will take before my time there becomes a faded scar etched into my memory like the white lines on my skin.

Things move even slower than I'm used to in those first few weeks, and for some time I don't fight the daydreams about Iris or the beckoning that a blunted blade can bring. I don't care if they throw me back into Lime Grove and chuck away the key for good this time. My parents watch me with frustration and disappointment—"Why are you doing this? Why are you doing this, again?"—but I choose not to hear them. Like I said, I don't fight it. For quite some time I think that there's no fight left in me, just the torrents of anger and fear and hatred and love and emptiness and screaming-so-loudly-but-no-one-can-hear.

But, as usual, I'm wrong. There is fight in my veins and fight in my blood and I am a bigger and bolder person than I've led myself to believe. I've been led down the garden path, where thorns have snatched at my ankles and bindweed has choked my mind.

I'm not readmitted to Lime Grove. My medicine is changed so that I don't slobber like Brew or have muscle cramps in my unnaturally induced sleep. Jacob comes to see me. I am surprised by the relief I feel when he arrives.

The familiarity of him is therapeutic. He makes me talk to him about Iris and he listens to what I did; it takes time but eventually the monster becomes quieter and quieter and I'm able to sit on my bedroom floor with lies booming into my eardrums and laugh in their ugly faces and go on a five-mile run instead. It isn't about Iris, you see. It was never about Iris. It isn't about the girl I thought I'd murdered, because the mind can play tricks in the dark. Iris wasn't the reason I got ill, she was the trigger. Dr. Flores, Emma, Nurse Will, Dr. Chance, Jacob—they just tried to help me find the truth, but I found it by myself eventually.

If you want to know what happened to the weird and wonderful people that I met at Lime Grove, then I'm afraid I can't tell you about all of them. I don't know what happened to Elle or Harper. I don't know what happened to Patient Will; I suspect that he's still in the hospital, but maybe that's pessimistic. Perhaps he'll be prime minister in a few years' time. Alice slipped back into her anorexia and within six months she was back in the hospital with a tube scraped up her nose. Her next hospital stay was longer, and I didn't hear from her for a year. She's out now, though, and I don't think she'll go back to the hospital. It feels different this time. Jasper started eating breakfast, and he eats it every day now. He got an apprenticeship and a boyfriend. I still see him sometimes. We made a trip to Mrs. Moonshine's ice-cream parlor only the other day. He had sprinkles.

Toby helps, but he isn't my cure. There isn't a cure. Except me: I am the cure.

He can kiss me, we can kiss, he can laugh and tell jokes and run with me and tell me to stop hurting myself, but he can't make me stop it.

"I've stopped smoking," he says when I offer him a roll-up one day, the filter sitting between my lips.

"Really?" It sounds unlikely. I look at his tobacco-stained fingertips.

"As of yesterday. It isn't good for my running." He snaps out of his own habit with one momentary decision. I don't know how he does it. I shrug and finish rolling myself the cigarette, clicking the lighter and allowing passive smoke to furl into his nostrils. He doesn't flinch.

Things are changing.

It isn't an epiphany. It isn't like that. I don't wake up one morning and out of the blue see the light filtering through the curtains and hear the bubbling flow of the water feature outside and suddenly feel *alive*. That comes much later on, after each morning when I do leave the house even though I just want to hide in bed, after each shower when I clean my body twice over instead of slicing it to shreds with a slippery blade like I want to. After each day that I do not kill myself, and allow the pain to just be, because if I do not cling to it, it cannot destroy me. Only after being smashed and battered and knocked, like Iris on the riverbed, but getting up each time, can I say, "I am here, I am alive, and I am not an evil person," and believe it to be true.

I can't describe what it now feels like to be alive to

someone who has not drowned in the darkness. Being alive is raw, and so terrifying that sometimes I look back toward the time before, and the darkness beckons me to crawl back into its depths and grovel at its feet like I used to, and sometimes, tempted, I take a step back. But being alive is also so intensely beautiful and colorful and there are days when I can laugh until I cannot breathe and my stomach bursts with happiness.

I am proud because I killed my monster, then destroyed the evidence, and I annihilated the darkness that tried to kill me, I climbed one hundred barbed-wire fences and I escaped hopelessness.

I yearn for the madness of life and I hope you will, too.

Author's Note

Why I wrote this book

When I decided that I wanted to write a book, I was sixteen. I had recently been admitted to a psychiatric ward and was overwhelmed with too much time to fill and too many things to say bubbling in my head. I was frustrated with everything I was experiencing: being far from home, and the stigma and misconceptions surrounding what I and so many other young people were going through. Tamar was a character whose story had been blossoming in my brain for a long time, and I started to write *On a Scale of One to Ten*.

Whilst Tamar and the colorful people she meets are fictitious and very separate from my reality, we traveled similar jagged journeys to the start of the recovery that many believe, for a sufferer of borderline personality disorder, to be impossible.

From a personal standpoint, writing *On a Scale of One to Ten* was a cathartic experience where I could release the intense emotions I was grappling with and make sense of them. I'd like to think that the result is a book that feels real because the feelings Tamar has are real. Real to me, real to other teenagers, and real to those who have been touched by mental illness. Most importantly though, I wrote *On a Scale of One to Ten* because it brought strength to me, and I really hope it brings some glimmer of hope, strength, and fight to others going through darkness, too.

If you are feeling suicidal or are affected by the topics in this book, you are not alone. No matter what you're facing, asking for help is a sign of strength. The below organizations can help.

You can reach:

- The **National Suicide Prevention Lifeline** 24/7 at 1-800-273-8255. To speak to a crisis counselor in Spanish, call 1-888-628-9454.
- The **Crisis Text Line** 24/7 by texting "HOME" to 741-741.
- You can call **The Trevor Project,** an LGBT crisis intervention and suicide prevention hotline, 24/7 at 1-866-488-7386.

To find local resources in your area, visit **To Write Love On Her Arms** at twloha.com

For additional resources, see the **American Foundation for Suicide Prevention** at afsp.org/find-support/resources and **SAVE** (Suicide Awareness Voices of Education) at save.org.